The Baron's Box

by

Mary Ann Clark

ISBN: 1548794295
ISBN-13: 978-1548794293

Dedication

This book is dedicated to Edith Wyschogrod
who first taught me all the different ways people
have thought about death, dying, and the afterlife.

Acknowledgments

I believe everyone we've ever met and every experience we've ever had influences who we are and what we can imagine. Although *The Baron's Box* is not based on any known understanding of the afterlife, the Bardo and its guardians have been shaped by my studies of world religions and the gods, deities and spiritual beings who inhabit the human imagination.

I owe a special thanks to the members of my critique groups, Richard Boich, Judi Burke, Katherine Caccavale, Judith March Davis (*Pagoda Dreamer* and *It Seemed to Matter*), Edward Gates (*A Ranger's Time*), William Johnstone (*The Seventh Message*), Marian Powell, Dougal Reeves, and especially Jeff Zucker whose image of a shining temple on the hill was the springboard for my 2015 National Novel Writer's Month project that became this story.

Along the way friends have read and commented on portions of this story including Ron Bathgate, Nancy Oliker, Bob Park, Gretchen Phelps, Carol Sowards, Tefra Woodridge.

Of course, this work would never have been finished and published without the invaluable work of my editor, Heidi M. Thomas, and the cover art of Mariah Sinclair.

And finally, I owe special thanks to my spouse, Art Gorski who has supported me through all the twists and turns of our lives together. I couldn't have done any of this without you.

Contents

PART 1 THE EMPYREAN 1

Chapter 1 3
Chapter 2 6
Chapter 3 10
Chapter 4 14
Chapter 5 17
Chapter 6 21
Chapter 7 24
Chapter 8 27

PART II NETHER REALM 29

Chapter 9 31
Chapter 10 34
Chapter 11 37
Chapter 12 41
Chapter 13 46
Chapter 14 49
Chapter 15 52
Chapter 16 55
Chapter 17 58
Chapter 18 60
Chapter 19 64
Chapter 20 67
Chapter 21 70
Chapter 22 73
Chapter 23 76

Chapter 24 80
Chapter 25 83
Chapter 26 86
Chapter 27 90

PART III KORE'S TEMPLE 95

Chapter 28 97
Chapter 29 102
Chapter 30 106
Chapter 31 109
Chapter 32 113
Chapter 33 116
Chapter 34 118

EPILOGUE 123

About the Author 125

Bardo

Tibetan term referring to a state of existence
between one life and another.

PART 1 THE EMPYREAN

Houston Chronicle

June 20, 2010

Houston Executive Shot, Killed by Home Intruder

Daniele Hardte, CEO of HardTech Enterprises, a Houston-based software development company, was shot and killed in her home early Saturday.

Galveston police were called to the Hardte home near The Strand about 3:14 am. It appears the 48-year-old woman, who was alone, confronted an intruder as he tried to enter the house.

Preliminary information alleges two police officers found Juan Garcia standing with a gun over Hardte's body. When he refused to drop the gun, Garcia was shot by one of the officers. He remains in critical condition at University of Texas Medical Center Hospital in Galveston.

CHAPTER 1

I should have wondered who and where I was, but in those first moments I was content to drift. I sighed, caressed by gentle rocking of a boat on water and the soft blanket swaddling me against the slight breeze. Opening my eyes, I pulled myself into a seated position, moaning as a sharp pain shot through the left side of my chest. I was stiff as though I had been sleeping for a long time. I wrapped the blanket tighter. Its warmth comforted me.

From my seat, I watched a young woman row with slow, sure strokes. Her long dark hair danced around a face tinged blue in the starlight.

"We're almost there." Her tranquil voice reassured me.

We were heading toward a landmass, an island perhaps. Still lethargic, I watched the water slip by, unthinking and unconcerned, as though this was the most natural thing in the world. Of course it wasn't.

Before I wondered why I did not remember anything prior to waking up, we approached a dock. A gentle ridge rose behind it, hiding whatever lay beyond. My escort threw a line to an older woman who tied it to the pier. Then they helped me out of the boat. I looked at myself. I wore a simple white tunic and trousers and nothing else. No shoes, no underwear. I felt naked and vulnerable.

Where was I? What had happened? Who were these people? What did they want? I wrapped my arms around myself, like a small child lost in a foreign market.

"Karon, where's the other one?" The older woman frowned.

That name was familiar but I couldn't place it. Why was my mind so slow?

"This is the only one I have," Karon said.

"There were supposed to be two." The woman sounded annoyed.

Karon raised her hands in the universal sign for "I know nothing."

"I'll have to sort that out later," the other woman mumbled, as if to herself.

She untied the lines and waved Karon and her boat away. Then she turned to me. "Welcome, Sara." Putting her arm around me, she guided me down the pier. "Let's go, dear."

Sara? My name is Sara? That didn't seem right. "You have the wrong person." I stopped. When I tried to think of my name, nothing came. "Who am I? What's going on? What's happened?" Fear clutched my belly.

"You're disoriented. That's to be expected." The woman walked me forward, ignoring my questions.

I planted my feet, refusing to go farther. I wanted answers. The woman pressed against my back and I staggered. I realized how weak I was. Had I been sick? Hurt? Where was I? Where had I come from? Where was she taking me? All I could do was stumble along beside her.

At the end of the pier, a wide path led up and over the rise. Bushes and brambles menaced from the darkness. When we stepped off the pier, soft ground cushioned my bare feet. The woman took my hand, leading me forward. Like a recalcitrant child I dragged my feet, fighting against the woman's pull, but her grip was firm. As we continued forward, my legs grew stronger, my steps more sure.

We climbed up and over another rise. The pathway split. On the right side, it became steeper and narrower. Dark trees, bushes and brambles formed an ominous tunnel. The pre-dawn light barely penetrated. On the left was a more appealing path through soft green trees scattered around a clearing filled with bright flowers.

A pole sat at the junction between the two paths. Wooden signs hung on its arms. The left-hand sign pointed toward the meadow. It depicted a person sitting in front of a square structure I recognized as a loom. The other sign, pointing into the forest, had the image of an attacking wolf, eyes wide and teeth bared. Even though fear crept up my back and settled between my shoulder blades, I was drawn to the right.

The woman paused as if undecided. "We need to find your compeer, your companion. And you could use the time."

My companion? Need the time? I shook my head, confused and frightened. I pulled at the woman's hand, wanting to escape back to wherever I had come from.

Before I could utter my questions or make a move, the woman yanked my hand, then turned to face me. "My name is Aurora." Her voice was low. "I will be your guide. If you fight me, we will have a very unpleasant time together. Do you understand, dear?"

Anger flashed through me as I stared at her. "No, I don't." I wanted answers, but I sounded like a petulant child. "What's happened?"

"We'll talk later." She pulled me away from the forest, toward the light and the flowering meadow. "Come along, now."

My ire evaporated in relief. We weren't continuing into the dark woods that both drew and repelled me. I imagined wolves similar to the one on the sign waited to attack and kill us. I wasn't prepared for that.

The sun slipped up over the horizon as we approached the clearing. Light danced on the edges of the leaves and flowers. I heard birds greeting the day and calling to each other from the trees. As frightening as that forest appeared, this meadow seemed peaceful and reassuring. That place at the base of my neck relaxed. Maybe things weren't so bad after all.

Beyond the meadow, we came to a group of huts scattered around a central plaza. In the distance I saw rolling hills with faint trails climbing toward a dazzling white building on the top of the most distance ridge. Aurora led me through the village, which appeared abandoned at this early hour. We stopped in front of a hut. I took it in with a single glance — a simple structure, four adobe walls capped by a conical roof. The wall facing us had a geometric design of three green triangles above a red spiral over two undulating blue lines. A plain white cloth covered the doorway.

Aurora lifted the covering and motioned me to enter. A hole in the center of the roof illuminated the single room. A wide platform covered by blankets hung off the wall to my left. Next to the bed, several sets of white tunics and trousers hung on pegs. On the wall opposite the door a basin, a pitcher, and fluffy white towels sat on a wide shelf. In the center of the space, four straight-backed chairs surrounded a three-foot square wooden table.

Aurora reached into a bag slung over one shoulder and placed a notebook on the table. "Wash yourself. Then rest if you'd like. I will see what The Baron wants to do about your missing compeer."

I felt welcomed and comforted yet had a sense of foreboding. Something strange was happening, and it was time I found out what.

"You need to tell me what's going on. Right now." My voice sounded stronger, more demanding than earlier. I stepped forward, breathing my frustration into her placid face. "Where am I, and what am I doing here?"

The woman retreated a step but didn't appear intimidated by my belligerence. She turned to leave. Then faced me and pointed to the notebook. "Your first task is to remember. It may help if you write everything you know." Then she went through the doorway letting the cloth drop behind her. Fear replaced my anger. I remembered nothing.

CHAPTER 2

With Aurora gone, I explored the room. Everything appeared to be of good quality but with no labels or identifying marks. The book looked like those personal journals you can buy anywhere. The cover and the first page displayed the same set of symbols on the front of this hut. The same three green triangles, red spiral, and blue lines. But below this one, a skull leered above crossed long bones. The inside was blank.

I became conscious of the slick sweat covering my body. The walk from the pier had been more strenuous than I'd realized. I stepped to the shelf with its basin, dropped my trousers and slipped the tunic over my head. The pitcher held warm water with a slight earthy scent that reminded me of moldering leaves. As I washed, I inspected my body.

I saw a young woman, about twenty-five years old. My body was well formed, not muscular like an athlete but not flabby either. Breasts, waist, and hips were on the smallish side but proportional. No fat or obvious silicon enhancements. No visible injuries, scars or birthmarks, no tattoos or evidence of piercings. I found a small tender spot below my left breast. The slightest touch there sent a shooting pain into my chest. I pulled my hand away, surprised.

I had shoulder-length hair that appeared smooth and clean. When I pulled strands forward, they had a common brown tone. I seemed to be a generic female with no obvious identifying characteristics. But I didn't recognize this body as my own.

Without a mirror in the room, I could not see if I looked like myself. Who was "myself?" Would I even know my face? As I stood naked in that small room I realized I had no idea. Everything was unfamiliar, yet how did I know? I had no memories before waking up on that boat.

Aurora had called me "Sara." That was not my name. But I could not say my real name. What had happened?

Leaving my dirty clothes in a pile on the floor, I pulled a clean tunic and trousers from the wall. I would demand answers when Aurora returned.

I sat at the table, staring at the book. What did I know? I woke up some time ago — it must have been hours — in the pre-dawn dark, at the bottom of a shallow boat. Although I remembered nothing, I found no evidence of trauma, except that one tender spot. Had I been kidnapped, drugged, and taken away to this place? That implied I was an important person. But why did my body, this perfect body, look so wrong? I understood kidnappers calling me by a false name — didn't they do that with abducted children? But how did they give me a different body?

Searching through my amnesia, I closed my eyes and examined my feelings about myself. I should be older, with a more mature figure and the beginning of middle-aged spread. And bigger boobs. The thought flashed through my mind that I had bought and paid for those things, so where were they? Reaching my hand, under my tunic I ran my fingers below my breasts. No post-surgery scars.

I was not who I appeared to be. How could I explain that? This was not the work of simple kidnappers. Something must have happened. Something awful. An intense, visceral fear gripped me. I remembered a flash of light. A sharp pain piercing my chest near that tender spot. I could not breathe. Blackness engulfed me as I fell forward

My eyes snapped open when my head hit the table in front of me. At first I could not catch my breath. Then I panted as though I had run all the way up here from the pier. I touched that small place below my heart. Again, the shooting pain. No mark, no evidence of any injury. Yet I felt an agony, the desperate attempt to breathe, the collapse into darkness.

I could not sit still any longer. I stood up, intending to explore the world outside when Aurora pushed the cloth covering the doorway aside and led a strange woman into the room. Where Aurora was soft, maternal in her colorful flowing caftan, this person was a warrior, full of sharp lines and hard edges. She wore dark trousers, a tight fitting top, and a winged helmet like someone in a Wagnerian opera, a Valkyrie perhaps.

"*Setzen Sie* down, Sara," she commanded. "Vee need to talk."

Her Germanic accent confirmed my first thoughts. But, even in my state of amnesia, I realized no good conversation starts with "we need to talk."

I stood defiant for a moment then sat. Perhaps now I'd get my answers. The two women took the chairs on either side of me. I looked from one to the other. Was this the beginning of my kidnappers' interrogation?

"What do you remember, dear?" Aurora asked, her tone soft, caressing.

"N-nothing," I stammered, afraid of what these two intended for me. I was not going to tell them even the small things I had realized.

"That is not true." The Valkyrie leaned in toward me.

"It is." My voice sounded weak in my own ears. I sat up straighter. I would not let these people intimidate me.

"I don't know who I am or what you want." I started strong. "Or why you've brought me here, or... or anything..." I hated the way my voice trailed off.

"Her compeer is delayed," Aurora said, ignoring me. "Let me have her for a while."

I was surprised when the Valkyrie stood and stomped toward the door. "I need to work with her, as vell. Do not wait too long und make things more difficult." She left, dropping the cloth behind her.

I looked at Aurora. Tears welled up in my eyes, but I refused to let them fall. I could not reveal how much that woman scared me. I sat up straighter. I would stay strong.

After a pause Aurora said, "We aren't your kidnappers."

How did she know what I was thinking mere moments ago?

"But you can't leave this room without a guide. I'll be back later and we'll go for a walk. You have much work to do but first you need to remember."

Before I could answer, she stood. As she pulled cloth aside, she turned. "There's a pencil in the book. It may help if you write everything." The fabric dropped behind her.

For long moments I stared at the doorway. The covering looked flimsy. They pushed it open easily. What stopped me from doing the same thing and leaving this room?

Aurora said they were not kidnappers, but people would notice if I disappeared. Even now the police were probably searching for me. I wondered if it be better to try to escape or if I should wait to be rescued?

Sitting and waiting wasn't my style. I would save myself. Maybe I could find another boat at the pier and get away.

When I touched the cloth covering the door, it sent a mild shock up my arm and became immovable. I pushed and pulled to no avail. Every time my fingers contacted fabric, I got shocked again. After many tries, I gave up. I was a prisoner.

I went back to the table, picked up the book and looked at the symbols on the cover. What did they mean? The skull and crossed bones were the most obvious. Were these people pirates? That didn't seem right.

What did I know? It was all a jumble. The flash of light, the explosion in my chest, then darkness. The water. What was the boat person's name? Karon? I remembered a story from Greek mythology about Charon ferryman who carried the dead across the river Styx. Then, everything burst into focus. My memory of pain, then oblivion. The journey over the water, the path that split in two, one destination dark and sinister, the other bright, welcoming. The pain, the awareness of my life slipping away, the darkness.

My memory of… I could not say it. But I knew. My memory of dying.

I buried my head in my arms. Was it true? Was I in fact dead? A tear slid down my cheek. Then another. Then a torrent. I sobbed, lost, as confusion and frustration engulfed me.

This was not how I had imagined the afterlife. Where was the bright light with family welcoming me? Or the pearly gates? Old Saint Peter with the giant book? The angels with their harps? God?

After a long time, I sat up and dried my eyes on my shirtsleeves. Deep in my belly, I realized the truth. I had died and here I was. Outside this hut paradise with meadows and flowers and sunshine awaited. The other choice was the hellish forest.

I'd made it! I sensed I was lucky. I did not think I had been the sort of person who ended up in heaven. But here I was! No matter who I had been or what I had done, I had achieved this place of beauty and light. I was more than surprised at my good fortune.

And I could not have been more wrong.

CHAPTER 3

When Aurora returned, I showed her the notebook with what I figured out. First, I was dead — as hard as that was to believe. That I had arrived in heaven with a new, younger body and a kindly guide to help me negotiate my everlasting life. I wrote that last as a sop to Aurora. She had been mostly kind to me. I did not mention my surprise at how my afterlife was working out. I did not need to tell her everything. Besides, I would not risk losing this lucky break.

Aurora barely glanced at my notebook. "Now, it's time for you to learn more about the Bardo." As she held the cloth door covering aside for me, I tried to remember where I'd heard the word "Bardo" before. I should have paid more attention in my humanities classes.

Outside, small groups of men and women sat together talking and laughing. Their flamboyant clothing was so different from my simple tunic and trousers. And they all looked older than me. Some even were gray haired or balding. Since I achieved such a youthful and healthy-looking body, I assumed that everyone in heaven did too. No one sitting around the plaza was decrepit, but none were young like me. It felt I won the afterlife lottery.

Aurora led me to a nearby table. "These will be your guides." Was heaven so complicated I needed a handful of advisors? Or, it occurred to me, was I such an important person I deserved special attention? I smiled at them and how well my afterlife was working out.

Then I looked my guides. One was the sinister woman who came into my hut earlier. Aurora introduced her as the Valkyrie Sigrún.

Her form-fitting metal breastplate gleamed in the sunlight. I remembered that in Norse mythology Valkyries led warriors who fell in battle to Valhalla, their paradise. What was she doing in my heaven? I doubted I had been a soldier, and this was not Valhalla. I tried not to notice her scowl.

The other person Aurora introduced as Ankou, looked more promising. Even seated, he appeared to be a tall, thin man. He wore a long coat and a broad-brimmed hat. I could not see his face but his hands were bony, gaunt, not arthritic but old-looking.

What should I do? Shaking their hands did not seem right, and I realized in that instant, I did not want to touch either of the guides. When each nodded, I nodded in return, repeating their names, "Sigrún, Ankou."

"You have much work to do, young Sara." Ankou's deep voice belied his emaciated appearance. "Your life is holding you back. You have this singular opportunity to remember before you must move forward."

Before I had a chance to say that I remembered almost nothing, Aurora touched my shoulder. "You will remember, dear." Again she appeared to be reading my mind.

I wanted to question them about the work Ankou expected me to do. What did he mean, my life was keeping me back? Move on where? Was not I already in heaven, or was this an anteroom, a way station leading to my eternal hereafter? What did I need to remember?

Before I worked out my questions, Aurora pulled me away and led me through the small village. I stared like a tourist in an exotic location. For the first time I saw other young people, each dress in loose trousers and simple tunics. An older person in a more colorful or elaborate costume accompanied each of them. Although you could tell the younger people apart, they all appeared to be a generic white males or females. No one was thin or fat, tall or short. Everyone had plain, brown, shoulder-length hair, even the men.

The area consisted of groups of huts. Only the symbols painted on the buildings distinguished them from each other. I remembered passing through a meadow filled with blooming flowers on my way from the pier. Now a dark dense forest surrounded the village on every side. That seemed strange, but since I anticipated an eternity to find out, I could wait. Later, I thought, I would ditch Aurora and explore on my own. This was going to be fun.

"What is that?" I pointed to the mountain in the far distance with the glistening building that sparkled in the sunlight.

She did not respond my question. In fact, she acted as though she had not heard me.

My temper flared. I was not used to being ignored. I almost asked her again in a more demanding tone. But I took a deep breath. I was new here. I would get my questions answered, eventually. I would insist on it. For the moment the sun shone warm overhead, and I drew a deep breath. I would simply bask in the wonder of my afterlife.

A more elaborate building I missed when I'd first arrived stood to our right, on the edge of the little village. Aurora called it The Baron's Palace. A medieval castle complete with towers, a moat, and a huge gate with a guardhouse on each side, its size and bulk looked incongruous looming over the simple, square huts. It appeared abandoned — no people, no flags flapping in the wind, no movement of any kind. It was well on its way to becoming a ruin. That seemed strange. You would not expect a decaying structure in heaven, but there it was.

On the other side of the village, Aurora pointed out an open-air pavilion with columns holding a roof overhead. People sat in front of looms making gorgeous Persian-style rugs. Was this the job Ankou expected me to do? I didn't ask but felt that my life had not prepared me for manual labor. Did this place need managers? That seemed more likely to have been my work, before.

An arena lay beyond the pavilion. Sigrún or another Valkyrie — they looked the same — was teaching people to use various archaic weapons: swords, bows and arrows, and the like. I found the idea of learning martial arts training appealed even if Sigrún frightened me. She and I needed to come to an understanding. Once she knew that I could not be intimidated, we would get along fine.

Aurora and I ended our tour with a stroll through a park between the pavilion and the arena. Its formal paths and the fountain in the middle reminded me of an English garden. She led me to a secluded area with a bench. Before we sat side-by-side, she picked a peach from a tree and handed it to me. I realized no one had offered me any food or drink since I'd arrived. I was not hungry, but I took it, smiling my thanks.

The fruit looked luscious but when I took a bite, it was so bitter I spit it into my hand.

"This isn't ripe." I handed it back to her.

Aurora frowned. "Finish it."

I shook my head. The astringent tang dried up my mouth.

"Finish it." Aurora's stern tone and hard look didn't allow for much of a protest. I bristled, then seeing no alternative, I obeyed. I gagged several times, but nothing came up. I was grateful for my empty stomach.

When I finished, I held the peach pit in my hand. Bits of fruit clung to it.

"Suck it dry," Aurora said, as I looked around for a place to dispose of the thing.

I shook my head. I had done well to eat as much as I did.

"Suck it dry," Aurora repeated, hard steel in her voice.

I put it into my mouth. The peach had been bitter, but the pit burned my mouth, my tongue, my lips. I glanced at Aurora who had been kind until now.

She looked back, emotionless.

I sucked until I removed the fruit. The acrid flavor diminished and then disappeared. When the pit was a tasteless lump, I spit it into my hand. It was clean and dry. I held it out to Aurora, and she took it.

"The taste of the fruit is the taste of the life you've left behind. This will help you remember and release so you can move forward."

I stared as she pulled a green string from a pocket and threaded it through a hole near one point of the pit. What did she mean, "remember and release"? I felt lucky to have realized I was dead. What else did I need to recall and why? Everything before I woke up on that boat was still a blank. Was not my life over, done?

She handed the seed on its string back to me. "Put it on. It is time for you to begin your journey."

CHAPTER 4

Aurora and I walked back through the garden. The seed hung above the neckline of my tunic. It stung where it touched my skin but when I tried to pull it away, she gave me a hard look.

"Don't." She gave no further explanation. I removed my hand, feeling like a disobedient child and hating myself for that weakness. I wasn't used to taking orders but for the moment I had no choice. When I remembered whatever I was supposed to remember and seized my freedom, Aurora would be sorry.

I followed her into the plaza where Sigrún appeared to be waiting for us. The two women nodded toward each other.

"She's all yours." Aurora turned to walk away.

I shuddered, wanting to call to her. I hated how Aurora had treated me, but I feared the Valkyrie. My heart pounded. *Don't leave me alone with this fiend.*

I flinched when Sigrún put her hand in the middle of my back. She forced me toward the pavilion.

"Do not fight me," she hissed when I tried to resist. I straightened my spine. I would do what she said until I could escape, but I didn't want her to think she intimidated me.

Other young people like me filled the open-air structure, each wearing simple white trousers and a tunic. Everyone sat in front of a large loom. Many moaned or even cried as they worked. A sinewy man wearing a leather vest and leggings stood in the back of the room.

Sigrún nodded to him and then pushed me toward an empty loom standing away from the others.

"*Sitzen Sie* here." She pointed to a low stool a little more than a foot high.

I crossed my arms in refusal. The man approached us, slapping a flexible rod against his leggings. My defiance flowed down my legs and puddled at my feet. I collapsed to the floor. Sigrún pushed me until I was kneeling in front of a stunning woven tapestry, my bottom resting on the stool. The piece in front of me was about three-fourths finished. It looked familiar, but I didn't have time to examine it.

"Pay attention." Sigrún squatted next to me and showed me how to untie the tiny knots holding the threads together. "This vill help you remember."

She loosened the first three or four knots for me and showed me how to bring the shuttle through the hole she created. The work appeared easy but tedious.

"Why?" How would undoing such a elegant tapestry would help me remember my life?

Sigrún ignored my question while flipping a length of soft white cloth over my knees. "You vill need this to keep your clothes clean. One of us vill return for you." She stood up and walked away. Before she disappeared out the door, I heard the slap of the foreman's rod behind me.

Pulling my attention back to the loom in front of me, I worked the shuttle through the remaining knots that Sigrún had loosened. This was not the work I expected to be doing in my afterlife. Wasn't heaven supposed to be free from such drudgery?

I looked around the room. Most looms were far enough apart to prevent conversation among the workers. The foreman moved away. He paced around the room, snapping his rod against his leggings. Louder moans traced his movements as he stopped to inspect the work, striking those who had apparently slacked off.

I looked back at my loom and loosened another knot as the man came toward me again. A sharp pain shot through my index finger. I pulled it away from the tapestry and put it in my mouth where I tasted the metallic flavor of blood. I touched the tapestry again and again. Each time a sharp pain accompanied by an involuntary yelp rewarded me. The threads were tiny razor blades slicing my clumsy fingers. I felt the bulk of the foreman behind me and heard the slap of the rod against his leggings. I held my breath, hoping he would move on, but he continued to stand there.

With a lighter touch I pulled at the thread and loosened the knot with only a pinprick. Cautiously, I untied the knots, touching the cloth on my lap to clean the blood from my fingertips. Soon, red spots sprinkled my lap cloth. When my attention drifted, I received a deeper wound and a larger spot of blood stained the fabric.

My close position prevented me from seeing the pattern of the tapestry. It wasn't a typical Persian design, but something more abstract. Perhaps it made more sense from a distance, but I had to focus to keep from being wounded.

The work was slow and painful. Loosening the tiny knots tormented my fingers. At first I refused to cry out or moan, but soon I was adding to the general keening. Would I spend eternity in this pavilion? I knew nothing of my life, but I did not think this was not the afterlife I imagined. Was I being punished for something I did not even remember? Anger roiled in my stomach as I tried to make sense of what had happened. With each movement, the sting of the seed on my skin reminded me of all the indignities I suffered.

I had seen the sunrise earlier, but now the light didn't appear to change. The only sign of the passage of time was the foreman's regular walks among the looms. I worked for hours with no relief or break. Once in a while a man or woman in colorful clothing took someone away from the pavilion. My initial anger dissolved into the monotony. I ached for Aurora to come for me. After a long while, I would have been happy to see Ankou or even Sigrún, anyone who would release me. But no one came.

I thought how I might get away from this place. The plaza was clearly visible, but there was no clear path out from where I sat. Before I was able to devise a plan, a young man in front of me stood up and sprinted away from his loom. In a moment, the foreman was next to him, his rod pressed against the man's back. The young man collapsed, writhing. Two guides appeared and led the him back to his seat. He continued to wail while they repositioned him. The slap of the foreman's rod against his leather pants brought me back to myself. Along with the other workers, I turned toward my tapestry. There was no escape.

For a long time I tried to concentrate on my work, ignoring the rest of the people. My thoughts flowed away as I narrowed my focus to the loom in front of me. I flinched when something touched my back. Without raising my head, I looked to the side at shabby shoes and dark, threadbare trousers.

"Come, young Sara." A bony hand pulled me to my feet, upsetting my seat. The bloody lap cloth fell to the floor. I reset the stool and folded the cloth over it as I had seen my fellow workers do. Then I followed Ankou, the gaunt guardian I had met earlier, out of the pavilion. As before, he wore a long dark coat and a broad-brimmed hat that hid his features.

My fingers and legs ached as I staggered behind him. Without looking back, Ankou led me through the plaza to my hut. He stopped at the doorway and held the cloth aside for me.

"Wash and put on clean clothes," he said. "The Baron is waiting."

I slipped into my room, grateful he didn't follow me. I may have been dead, but I still had a modicum of modesty.

CHAPTER 5

As we approached the Baron's Palace my first impressions were confirmed. It looked abandoned, derelict. Guardhouses stood on either side of the central gate, but no one greeted or challenged us. There were no sounds. No smells of cooking. No vehicles or any other people, only Ankou and me.

I had washed and put on a set of the clean trousers and a tunic. The walk across the plaza and the warm water on my skin had invigorated me. I had gotten no blood on my old clothes, but they were too wrinkled and shabby to wear any longer. Under my thin clothing, I still felt almost naked, but I had no other options. I smoothed my hair with a comb and brush I found next to the basin. Without a mirror I could not see myself, so I hoped I looked acceptable.

Walking with Ankou, I took a deep breath, pulling myself up until I was ready for anything. As we approached the palace, I thought something was about to change. He had saved me from the ugliness of the pavilion. The sun shone overhead. I had a lithe young body and all was well. It was a good day to be dead.

Without a word or slowing his pace, Ankou reached back and grabbed my hand in his bony fingers. His skin felt dry, almost dusty. We passed through the central courtyard and then entered the main building. At the end of the hallway I saw an ornate door several stories high with a small, human-sized door cut into the middle. Before we got there, Ankou turned and pulled me into a side room. It was not huge but well appointed. Tapestries covered the walls and plush Persian-style carpets were scattered across the floor. I noticed a faint musky odor. In front of us, on a raised platform, a black man in a tux with a white long-tailed jacket and top hat stood up to greet us.

Ankou pulled me toward the stage, then pushed me to my knees. Before I could get a better look at the person I assumed was The Baron, Ankou's bony hand forced my head to the floor. It took a moment to realize that he was resting one foot on my neck. I tried to push myself up but his weight was solid.

"Baron," Ankou said, obeisance in his voice.

"Ankou, I see you have brought us a new soul." The Baron's drawl sounded familiar. *New Orleans* flashed through my mind. Had I lived there? I didn't remember. "Let her up."

Ankou removed his foot and used my hair to draw my head up and back so I sat geisha-style on my knees. His grip was firm but not painful. I was lucky to have landed on the edge of a rug, instead of on the stone floor. I pulled myself tall, summoning my feelings of well-being and composure. Whoever lived here must be important. I wanted to make a good impression.

The elegant man in front of me looked younger than Aurora and the other guides. Instead of a traditional tux shirt and bowtie, he wore a white silk shirt opened well below the breastbone, exposing his muscular chest. A necklace of small bones and teeth filled the space. A purple cummerbund and ornate walking stick completed the ensemble. The left side of his face had been subtly dusted with a white powder giving him both an appealingly exotic and terrifying appearance.

Butterflies fluttered in the pit of my stomach. He captivated my imagination. For a moment, I envisioned tracing a well-manicured fingernail down his beautiful chocolate-brown pecs and into the terrain below. I saw the two of us romping on a gorgeous silk-sheeted bed, exploring each other's bodies. I shivered. Here was someone who could release me from the torment of the pavilion and turn my afterlife into a pleasure. And, I thought, I could make it worth his time. For a second, I wondered where that idea came from, but somehow I knew how to get what I wanted from a powerful man. With a practiced movement, I tilted my head down and to the side, then looked up at him in a way that drove men wild.

"Welcome to the Bardo, the realm of the dead" The Baron's placid face showed no hint of welcoming.

My daydream shattered into a thousand shards and I cringed. There was that word again. I had never heard of the Bardo. But as I ran my tortured fingers along the cloth of my trousers, I realized this was not the heaven I had first imagined. Perhaps The Baron was not who he appeared to be either.

"You must remember and release your past life before you can move forward." The Baron tapped his walking stick on the floor. "Your compeer, your companion, is arriving. You two will continue together. Use this delay to prepare. My guides can help you."

Although his cool manner disappointed me, The Baron was the first person I met here whom I wanted to get to know better. I decided he was the companion I wanted. He appeared rich and potent, maybe the most important man here. Wanting him to think of me as more than just another one of his subjects, I added a mysterious and suggestive Mona Lisa smile to my look. Then, I licked my lips. I understood how to attract a powerful man.

My pulse quickened as The Baron came down the steps and stood over me. I tried to scoot backward so I could gaze up at him but discovered Ankou's legs against my back. I looked up through my lashes, imagining The Baron extending his hand, inviting me to join him.

Instead, he cupped the back of my head and pushed until my forehead pressed against his shoes. I gagged from the faint odor of decaying meat. The bitter fruit I had eaten earlier rose to the back of my throat.

"Don't toy with me." His voice was a heavy door slamming shut.

After a moment, the force of his hand eased and his shoes disappeared. Wait, I wanted to say. Don't leave me like this.

Someone touched my shoulder. When I raised my eyes, only Ankou remained in the room. He helped me to my feet, took my hand, and led me into the hallway. He didn't even seem to notice I resisted and pulled against him. As we walked through the courtyard and out of the castle, I wondered what I needed to do to come back here, alone. Perhaps The Baron was playing hard to get. I felt the attraction. I knew I could change my circumstances if I returned without an escort.

"What did you learn about your past life at the workshop, young Sara?" Ankou asked as we walked across the courtyard and out the front gate.

"The workshop?" My fantasy evaporated.

"The building with the tapestries. What have you learned?"

I stumbled, but his grip on my hand kept me from falling. When he turned, I saw his face. No wisps of hair peeked out from under his hat. No eyebrows, no mustache, or beard. Thin lips revealed vile teeth. To say he was skeletal was an overstatement. His head looked like a skull covered with translucent skin.

"I-I don't think I learned anything." A shudder rippled though me. "That is a cruel place. I refuse to go back there." I tried to express my indignation, but my voice sounded whiny.

Ankou didn't respond but led me through the village toward the pavilion.

"Please," I pulled on his bony hand, losing any dignity I had achieved, "please don't make me go there."

He dragged me through the door and to my loom. A clean towel replaced the bloody one I had left on the stool. I struggled in his grip, ready to escape and run away, but he pushed me. After a moment, I let him help me sit and arrange the cloth over my knees. Everyone in the room watched us.

"The story of your life is here." He waved at the tapestry in front of me. "The threads are painful because you made them sharp. Learn what you can, now, while you have this chance."

As Ankou left, I heard the foreman behind me tapping his leather trousers with his rod. There was no escape.

He let me work at a slower and more deliberate pace than earlier, so I had fewer cuts and less blood. When he walked away, I stopped working to search for any hint of my previous life. I leaned back to get a better view of what images might be hidden in the tapestry. But I was still too close. The swirls of colors ran together. I gave up on the larger picture and moved forward to focus on the individual knots. I reached up to untie the next one.

CHAPTER 6

"He's not a bad sort," said a soft voice from a loom less than a foot away from mine.

"What?" I whispered.

"Volos, the foreman. He's trying to help us resolve our former lives, but it's hard for some."

I turned toward the woman sitting next to me. Like me she was a generic female, mid-twenties, brown hair, dark eyes, wearing white trousers and tunic with a towel dropped across her knees. Unlike my cloth, hers was almost pristine, with only a couple small spots of blood.

She smiled at me. "They call me Sara."

"Me, too." I smiled back at her.

"Everyone's a Sara," she explained. "Except, of course, the guys. They're all called Sam. I guess our old names aren't important anymore."

I nodded toward Volos, the foremen. "He looks nasty. Mean. I've seen him beat people with that stick of his."

"So have I," my new friend said, "but I've seen him be kind, too."

I raised my eyebrows.

"Like now. He watched you for a long time and then walked away. He could see you weren't daydreaming."

I agreed. I had expected a blow, but it never came.

"Shush." She turned toward to her loom.

There was a commotion behind us. Volos struck someone who fought back. It took three people to break up the fight. In moments, we watched a Valkyrie march the man out. Then we all focused on our work with less moaning and crying.

So everyone here is not passive and compliant. I felt better about my attempts to defy Aurora and the other guardians. Of course, the man's rebellion had not worked for him. I expected he would be back in front of his tapestry soon. My acts of defiance had not worked either. Here I was again facing this dreadful loom attempting to recall whatever I was supposed to remember.

I pulled at a couple more knots, trying to avoid hurting myself. When Volos moved to the other side of the room, I pushed myself back on my bench to get a wider view of the tapestry. If it told the story of my life, I could not see it.

"Psst," the Sara next to me whispered. "Don't try to grasp the whole thing at once. Look for individual scenes." She pointed to an area she had almost finished. "I am working backwards from my death." She held her thumbs and index fingers together to make a small square then moved her hand along the bottom of her tapestry. "I don't understand it yet." She picked at another knot. "That's why I'm still here. They said when I have unraveled my life story, I'll be able to release it and move on."

Before I tried making a movie of the images in front of me, I heard Volos moving in our direction, slapping his rod on those leather trousers. I went back to picking at my tapestry, pulling out one small knot at a time.

My death. I was so concerned about who I was before I came here, I had not thought about my death, the event that brought me here. Nobody wants to consider their death. We all want, wanted, to think it would never happen to us. Was this workshop my hell for eternity? Picking out knots on a tapestry, cutting myself over and over again on the threads? Always under the threat of Volos? But The Baron said after I remembered I could continue on. Whatever that meant. Now, my new friend told me the same thing. Once she understood her life story, she could move forward. Maybe there was a way out of this torture.

Again I considered what I knew. I had no real information, only my feelings and intuitions. Everyone here that was not a guide seemed the same age I was. So how I looked not did indicate how old I was when I died. There was that word again. I ignored my discomfort and pressed on.

I felt as though I was older than this body. But I was not surprised to see I was female when I washed myself. So I guessed I had been a more mature woman. That's all I could figure out as I picked at those knots.

I worked at the knot along the bottom edge of my tapestry. When Volos moved to another part of the workshop, I stopped working and looked again at the splashes of color.

"Psst," my friend whispered again. "Find the last scene. It's your birth or your death or the pivotal event of your life. When you find it, it's supposed to trigger your memories so you can begin your transition."

I examined the far right edge of my work. I held out my left thumb and index finger in an "L" and moved them back and forth. When I blocked out the rest of the tapestry, that little corner became clearer to me. It wasn't a scene but a burst of colors, patches of red and black with bright yellows and oranges behind them. I stared at the area, but still nothing came to me.

Disgusted, I returned to picking knots. Losing my concentration, I cut my index finger. I pulled it away from the tapestry. Touching it to my lap cloth, I tried to staunch the flow. But it left a bright red pool in the middle of the towel. This was the deepest gash so far and I could not get it to stop bleeding. How could a dead person have so much blood?

I held the fabric against my finger. When it finally stopped running, I was leery of going back to work, afraid I would re-open the wound and bleed all over the tapestry. What would Volos do then? Would he even notice?

A guide I didn't recognize came and took the woman next to me away, and I wondered how long I had been sitting here. The sun overhead had not moved. Was it always mid-morning here?

I heard Volos walking toward my side of the workshop so I tried working without using my index finger. That made me even clumsier. I looked at the messy lap cloth. There was a blotch with a streak running into one corner and splatters over the rest of it. If I didn't know better, I would have thought someone had been shot here.

As I sat back to look at the images, the peach pit brushed against my chest and a sizzle of pain ran through me. When I held up my fingers, the image was clearer. I realized that the red on the tapestry, like the red on my lap cloth, represented a bloodstain. Maybe there had been an explosion. Were the yellow and orange tones a fire? No, a gunshot. The black, which looked like a smudge earlier, now had the vague shape of a handgun. Had I been shot? Had I been murdered? If I was a victim, why was I in this hell, picking at this horrible tapestry, cutting myself to shreds?

I threw the lap cloth on the floor, intending to storm out of this place, find Aurora, and get answers. Before I could stand up, I felt a strong hand on my shoulder.

"Be careful, young Sara," Volos said, his deep voice holding me on my bench. "Here comes your guide now."

I looked up. Sigrún was stomping toward me, her eyes flashing

CHAPTER 7

Sigrún stalked across into the pavilion in full battle dress, with the metal breastplate and winged helmet she had been wearing earlier. She had added leather leg guards and a sword hanging in a worn scabbard. She grabbed my hand and yanked me to my feet. Without a word, she dragged me from the workshop and path toward the arena where Aurora and I had seen people training.

I had just learned that I was a murder victim. Why was she treating me this way? Why was I being made to endure this hell? Didn't I deserve better treatment? I did not need to take this abuse any longer. It was time I stopped being pushed around and got real answers.

I planted my feet and yanked backward, pulling my hand free. "Stop." My tone of authority surprised me. Where had I learned to talk like that? "Stop this, right now."

Sigrún turned. The anger on her face made me think my act of protest was too much. But I wasn't about to back down.

"I'm not going anywhere with you." I turned away.

"Sara." Sigrún reached toward my hand.

I retreated beyond her reach then ran as fast as I could through the plaza.

When I arrived at my hut, I found Aurora sitting on a bench to the right of the doorway.

"What's going on, Sara?" She stood up and touched the door covering. The soft cloth stiffened. I did not have to touch it to know it would not open for me.

"Let me in." I extended my hand toward the door.

"No. First we talk." She sat down and patted the seat next to her.

I glared. "Why am I here? Why are you people torturing me?"

"Sit, dear." Her quiet voice defused my anger.

"Unlock my door."

Aurora smiled at me, reached over and pulled back the cloth.

I considered escaping into my hut but realized this was my first real opportunity to get answers to my questions. As I moved to sit on the bench, I noticed my notebook was there. When I picked it up, it felt warm.

"Did you learn something at the workshop, child?" Aurora asked as if she didn't know everything that happened. It was obvious she had read the few things I had written. I opened the notebook and flipped through the pages. After my last note was the same image I had seen on the tapestry.

I frowned. "What does this mean?"

"What do you think?" Aurora responded.

I pointed to the red patch. "This is blood, a lot of blood. This is a gun, and behind everything, the blast of the shot."

She nodded, encouraging me to continue.

"I was shot and bled to death. I'm an innocent murder victim, and you're treating me as if I was the murderer." When I caressed the pit hanging from my neck, its sting comforted me in some perverse way.

"You're right as far as you go," she said, "but that's not the whole story. You need to learn more."

I shook my head. "No, I'm not going back to that loom." I held out my hands, showing her the small scab where I had cut myself. "You can tell me. Right now."

"I can't do that, child," she said. "I know you hate the loom but I can't tell you, you have to remember. The more you remember here, the easier the rest of your journey will be."

I kept shaking my head. Never would I let her or anyone, drag me back to that instrument of torture. "I won't." I was determined to win this battle.

"You need to remember your story." Aurora looked me in the eye. "And the loom can help you. You created the sharp edges of your threads. You can soften them. Each drop of your blood is a bit of polish smoothing out the sting of your life."

My resolve collapsed. "Why?" Tears welled up in my eyes. "Why must I go back? Why must I cut my fingers to shreds unraveling that dreadful tapestry?"

Aurora patted my wrist. Then she scooted over and put her arm around my shoulder. "The part of the Bardo, the Empyrean is a way station." She waved her arm indicating the surrounding huts. "You can't stay here. Soon you will have to move on. You have a unique opportunity while we wait for your compeer. When you remember, you won't repeat the callousness of your past."

I looked at the notebook on my lap. Blank pages stared back at me. What kind of person had I been for this gentle woman to accuse me of being callous? Could I learn more by returning to the loom?

I tried one last gambit. "Then keep Sigrún away from me. And Volos, too. I will do what I need to do but not if they are threatening me."

Aurora shook her head. "Your compeer is on his way and you have to get ready."

I wondered about this so-called compeer. But before I could question her, Aurora continued, "You have a fierce spirit, dear, and Sigrún can help you prepare for the challenges ahead. You need to work with her, learning the way of the warrior. You will do great things if you learn the disciplines of the Valkyrie."

I heard the admiration in her voice, even as fear of Sigrún roiled in my abdomen. Maybe I wasn't all bad. Maybe I could overcome whatever atrocities I had committed. Pushing myself back on the bench, I sat up straighter. I would not be a pawn of these so-called guides. I was a strong person with a fierceness of spirit, not some sniveling victim that died for nothing.

As if summoned by our conversation, Sigrún crossed the plaza and strode up to my hut. Her long legs made a solid but silent connection with the earth. Aurora moved her arm from behind me and slid away so our bodies no longer touched.

"Are you ready, young Sara?" Sigrún looked fierce with her armor and sword but her voice sounded softer now. She seemed less like a demon and more like an older sister come to take me into her realm. She held out her hand. I stood and looked back at Aurora for a moment. Then trying to match Sigrún's stride, I went with her across the plaza and past the workshop toward the arena where I would begin my training.

CHAPTER 8

Sigrún walked straight to the armory where she pulled down two wooden swords as long as my arm and handed me one. The sword was heavy but well-balanced in my hand.

"You vant to fight. Let us see how good you are."

She led me away from the armory and into an open field. No part of me seemed skilled in swordplay, but I was angry enough to engage Sigrún and anyone else she might pit against me.

The Valkyrie must have realized I didn't know how to use a sword. Standing behind me she pushed and pulled my arms and legs into a fighting stance. The pose felt familiar. Had I had some martial arts training? Maybe I did know something about this.

She walked around to stand in front of me. "You vant to hurt me. Go ahead and try."

Thinking I could put a quick end to this, I turned my sword and swung at her neck. She parried my blow and came at me. It didn't take long before I realized my problem. Not only was she trained, but she was wearing a helmet, a protective breast plate, leg and arm guards. I had no more protection than my simple cloth tunic and trousers. Soon deep bruises covered my arms, legs, head, neck, and torso. She never broke the skin, but each hit convinced me of my ineptitude.

When every part of me was sore and bruised, she raised her sword. "Stop."

I dropped my arm, exhausted, grateful for this session to be over.

"I can see you had some training," she smiled, "but obviously not enough."

Then she showed me a series of movements, stylized fighting poses. Some felt familiar, others were not. She ran me through the poses over and over again. When I missed the form or tried to stop she smacked me with the flat edge of her sword. When I completed the entire sequence without a mistake or misstep, she lowered her weapon.

"Taken *Sie* a moment," she said. "Then ve vill try again."

Before I caught my breath, she resumed her fighting stance. I followed and again we fought. Now that I had learned the poses, I could at least defend myself against some of her blows. I even got past her defenses and landed a blow or two of my own.

When we stopped again, she taught me an additional series of poses. I realized that while the first set was defensive, these moves were offensive. Again she ran me through the sequence over and over again, hitting me with her sword when my energy flagged or I missed the form. After another short rest period, we fought again. This time I felt both my offensive and defensive moves showed more confidence. I seldom got past Sigrún's own defenses, but both my form and my skills improved. And I became a more disciplined fighter.

When we stopped, Sigrún took me back to the armory and replaced my sword with a long, wooden dagger. It was well balanced but only half the length of the sword. We returned to the practice field where she taught me a new set of poses. This series was designed for a person with a dagger facing an opponent with a longer weapon. These were much more difficult. A person with a dagger is always at a disadvantage against a sword. But I learned techniques that equaled out the odds, and when we sparred I fought better than I had expected.

At the armory I returned my practice weapon. Bruised, and with my clothes in tatters, I was exhausted but also exhilarated. This had been the most satisfying time I had spent since coming to the Empyrean. For all that Sigrún bested me at every turn, I no longer feared the Valkyrie. Instead I felt a new rapport as though we were part of a sisterhood. She let me slip my arm into hers as she led me back to my hut.

PART II NETHER REALM

Houston Chronicle

June 28, 2010

Shooting Victim Dies in Local Hospital

Family and friends of Houston resident Juan Garcia gathered yesterday to bid farewell to their husband, father, and colleague. Garcia was shot in an altercation at the home of HardTech Enterprises CEO Daniele Hardte. The Garcia family, insisting that Mr. Garcia had not killed Hardte, kept him on life-support while police investigated the incident. Police now say Garcia was the victim of a case of mistaken identity when he approached Hardte's mansion Saturday. Hardte was shot and killed during the ensuing fight. Garcia was shot by responding officers.

CHAPTER 9

Sigrún had been a hard taskmistress. I was surprised to discover I knew some martial arts and improved as we fought. She did not hold back. Although the blows of her sword hurt, nothing seemed broken, and since I was already dead, there was only so much real damage she could cause. I felt strong and capable to a level that surprised me. I must have been older when I died. At least I expected my body to react like an older person's. I was filled with a deep visceral pleasure when it did not.

"Clean up and change," Sigrún said as we approached the door to my hut. My clothes were filthy, my hair was filthy, I was filthy. "Aurora will be by soon to escort you back to the workshop."

I twisted my mouth at the thought of returning to the loom. All I wanted was the comfort of a warm bath, a meal, and good night's sleep. Throughout this long day — were there days in the afterlife? — I had not eaten more than that bitter peach. In spite of the intense workout I had endured, Sigrún had not offered me a sip of water. I was not hungry or thirsty. But I was tired. Ever since I first realized I was dead, my guides had hustled me from one event to another without a break or respite of any sort. Hadn't I done enough? Couldn't I rest? What's the point of all this? The loom? The training?

Sigrún pulled the cloth aside and pushed me into the hut. "Don't dawdle," she said before I could protest.

As she dropped the door covering, I noticed a subtle difference in the room. It had a new, strange, masculine aroma. A pair of trousers and shirt were missing and a second notebook sat on the table. It had the same green triangles, red spiral, and blue waves as mine. But where my book had an image of a skull and crossed bones, this one's skull was softer, more childlike, with angel wings.

I stepped to the table to get a better look. When I touched the book, electricity flashed from it to my fingertips, my poor abused fingertips. I could almost hear the command, "Don't touch." I stared at the notebook for a long moment and then turned away. One more mystery without an answer.

Moving to the ledge, I dipped my hand into the basin. As before, the warm water was the perfect temperature. Letting my trousers fall to the floor, I pulled the tunic over my head. I cleaned away the sweat and grime from my training session, working around the peach pit hanging at the top of my cleavage. The thing was supposed to remind me of my life, but I remembered almost nothing. Its tiny pin pricks whenever it touched my skin were simply one more irritant.

I would have preferred a bath, or even a shower, but I found this form of washing comforting. By the time I finished, my bruises and underlying soreness had disappeared. My exhaustion left, and I felt fit and whole again.

I couldn't see a way to shampoo my hair. After slipping into a fresh set of trousers and tunic, I reached for the brush. After a moment, I realized that the dirt evaporated as I brushed. Soon my hair returned to its smooth silky texture.

Clean and dry, I felt stronger, more in control of myself. I was proud of the progress I had made under Sigún's tutelage.

Did heaven have an army? What enemies threatened the Empyrean? I thought about that mysterious forest surrounding our little village. What monstrosities hid in that darkness? Aurora said I had a warrior spirit. Now Sigún was teaching me how to fight in this new place.

Maybe Sigrún would let me leave the workshop behind and join her troops. As I remembered it, the Valhalla of myth was a place of feasting and carousing. I found the image of a room full of powerful, tipsy men exciting. Besides, a strong warrior woman would be respected in such a place. I was still a novice, but I had shown I was a fast learner. I imagined myself leading a band of warriors out into that forest to fight whatever evil lurked there.

For the first time since I woke up on that boat, I felt good, in control of my life… er, afterlife. Although not athletic-looking, this body had proved both agile and powerful. I had learned the moves Sigrún taught me and used them when we sparred. I had come back to my hut exhausted but enlivened. I looked forward to returning to the arena and continuing to work with the Valkyrie. Why did I need to return to the pavilion with its hateful looms?

I returned to the table to write up my experience in my notebook. Instead, after the intensity of my training, the warm bath, and the rhythm of my hair brushing, I fell into a sort of trance. I saw myself, at least I think it was myself. I was in a huge house, almost a mansion, sitting on a wide street with similar houses on either side. In this dream-like state, I saw a woman asleep in a king-sized bed with soft cream-colored bedding. Outside the window, the night was dark and moonless. I slipped into the sleeping form, becoming the woman in the bed.

I am startled awake by someone pounding on the front door of my home. Who is knocking at 3:00 in the morning? I open the drawer and pull out a pistol. It is comfortable in my hand. This is my gun.

"Sara." Aurora pulled aside the door covering, startling me from my daydream. The sudden movement bounced the peach pit against my chest, sending tingles through me.

Had I envisioned part of my past life? What had happened?

"Are you ready, dear?"

I shook myself awake. Then sat up straighter, my newfound strength pushing me to resist.

"I'm not going back there." If I could return to my dream, I could learn more about my previous life without having to endure the torture of the loom. Besides, I was a warrior, soon to join Sigrún's forces.

Aurora smiled and held out her hand. I knew she would not let me off so easily. My fantasy of joining the Valkyrie on an exciting adventure shattered. My time with Sigrún had been a welcome diversion, but there was no escaping the loom. I stood up and slipped my left hand into hers. The ghost-weight of the gun sat like a whisper in my right.

CHAPTER 10

When I was again settled at my loom and Aurora left the workshop, I realized that a man had replaced the woman who befriended me earlier. He was about my age with shoulder-length brown hair. Sam — all the men were named Sam — wore the white trousers and shirt that were the uniform of this place.

He stared at his loom, weeping. He had done no work. Only a few of the knots were loosened and no blood stained on his lap cloth. I glanced around and spotted Volos on the other side of the workroom. The man was lucky. Volos often punished those who sat and cried in front of their looms.

I was sorry the friendly woman was gone. She had helped me figure out why I was here. This Sam looked even more ignorant than I was. He could not help me.

I put my thumbs and index fingers together to form the open square as my friend had taught me. I recognized the moment I had identified before my time with Sigrún. The gun took on the shape of the pistol in my daydream.

Moving my hands to the left to isolate the previous event, the image of two people appeared. I saw a man and a woman standing by open door. Their arms were around each other. Were they embracing? Dancing. It was dark. Was it night?

I moved my hands to the next earlier scene. It was a swirl of color. Perhaps I needed to understand this couple before the previous scene revealed itself.

When I took my hands away, I could make out both scenes. I picked the next knot. Ankou said I made the threads sharp. Did that mean I could blunt them? I continued unraveling the last image, what I thought of as my death scene. As I tried to maintain a light touch on the knots, I considered the relationship between the moments. Were the people lovers? Why would they be embracing otherwise? But if they were, how did one of them, me, get killed? Did they have a quarrel? I attempted to imagine myself arguing with someone with a gun. That seemed foolhardy. But I had died. And he was the person who killed me.

I looked at the couple again. The woman had blond hair trimmed into rumpled pixie cut. She wore a long revealing gown that emphasized nicely formed breasts. She didn't look like me. Or rather, I didn't look like her. Maybe nobody here looked as they had in life. The more I stared at her the more I felt a bond. If the tapestry portrayed the truth, this was what I had looked like.

I focused on the man I assumed to be my killer. He was shorter than the woman, with jet-black hair, a little too long in the back. And he wasn't dressed as elegantly as the woman. Instead, he wore blue jeans, a gaudy work shirt, and bulky boots. As I looked closer, they didn't appear to be a couple at all but strangers. Had he grabbed her? Attacked her? Had he come to rob her?

As I picked at the knots, I remembered my daydream and tried to connect it to the scenes in the tapestry. In my dream, someone had awakened me in the middle of the night. The dress in the tapestry could be a nightgown. I had taken a firearm out of the drawer. Had a stranger shot me with my own gun?

Zap. A sharp pain raced through my right shoulder and down my arm toward my fingers. I yelped. I had not noticed Volos had returned to our side of the workshop.

He stood behind me, slapping the rod on his leather pants. I rearranged the cloth that had slipped from my lap, then reached into the tapestry. My fingertips were so numb I no longer felt the threads cutting me.

I untied several knots before Volos walked away.

"Are you all right?" the man next to me whispered. "What happened?"

"Yes. Yes, I think so." I untied another knot and then looked to be sure Volos was too far away to notice us talking.

"I figured out something about my death, and Volos didn't like it." I don't know why I said that, but why else would he have zapped me? I thought I had been doing the real work of this place: learning about my past life.

"It's strange being dead, isn't it?" he asked. "I think I left behind a family, a wife and a couple of kids. They will have a hard time without me." His eyes filled with tears. "I didn't mean to die."

Before I could respond, a guide walked up to the man's loom. This guide was beautiful in a masculine sort of way. Tall and slender with well-formed arms and legs, broad shouldered but narrow at the hips. Like Sigrún, he wore a breastplate and guards on his shins and forearms. But where Sigrún looked sinister, he was gorgeous in his golden armor. I would have followed him anywhere. The stunning guide pulled the man up and led him away.

I returned to my tapestry and worked on another knot. As the next earlier image began to emerge, I realized I must have been right about the second scene. Trying not to stare as a new image shimmered and took form, I thought about the man's guide. How did he get an angel when I had a scowling Valkyrie?

I untied several knots before the whole scene solidified. I could see the buxom blond standing in the doorway, her gun pointed at the man who stood on her porch. Putting it together with my daydream, I understood that someone I didn't recognize had come to my house in the middle of the night. The size and elegance of my home suggested I was rich. He looked like a workman or some lowlife from the streets. I had opened the door with my weapon pointing at him. Instead of leaving, he rushed me, and we struggled. The gun went off. I was shot and killed. I couldn't tell who pulled the trigger, but I blamed him.

I wished I had brought my notebook with me. I needed to write down what I had learned. I hoped Aurora would come for me soon and I could share what I had learned. I knew how I had died. I sighed. Maybe now I could leave this place.

But no one came for me. I kept untying knots at the slowest pace I thought Volos would allow, knot after knot until I had untied the whole bottom row of the tapestry. Those last three scenes had come in clearly, but no more revealed themselves. I still knew nothing about my life before I was killed.

The man next to me had wept for the family he left behind. Did they weep for him as well? Did I have a family that wept for me? Where were the scenes of my family, my friends?

"*Kommen Sie*, Sara."

I looked up. Sigrún stood between my loom and the man's. She held out her hand. I got up, folded the lap cloth and put it on the stool. I would have preferred to talk to Aurora, but I was glad to see even Sigrún. Perhaps she had come to continue my training.

"Your compeer, your companion, has arrived," she said as we approached the arena. "You vill be leaving soon and you are not ready. You have much to do."

She led me into a shed full of weapons, pulled a long dagger off the rack and handed it to me. "You vill need to use this und use it vell."

A buzz of energy shot up my arm as my hand closed around the grip. I didn't have time to wonder why, if I was already dead, I needed to learn to use such a weapon. Fear shot through me.

CHAPTER 11

I spent a long time working with Sigrún in the arena, learning to use the dagger. It didn't need the strength or finesse of the swords I used earlier. When she released me, my fear receded. I felt confident in my abilities. Before she led me to my hut, she gave me a scabbard for the dagger.

Once she dropped the cloth over the door, I stripped off my filthy clothes. The second notebook that had been on the table before was gone. Had I imagined it?

Again, I washed myself and brushed out my hair. As I pulled on the last clean pair of trousers and tunic from the hooks, Aurora and Sigrún arrived.

"Tell me what you know," Aurora insisted.

I told her the story of my death, as I understood it. She nodded but shook her head as I hypothesized my death.

"Keep this with you." She handed me the notebook. "You haven't learned everything you need to know yet." My hope for leaving this place vanished. She was sending me back to that awful loom.

Sigrún handed me a bag that appeared to have been cut from my tapestry. Then she stepped back to look at me.

"You are as ready as I can make you." She shook her head. Then they turned and left. When I tried to follow, the door covering had turned into a solid, immoveable barrier.

I set the bag on the table and then opened my notebook. I had much to record. After my last notes an image from my dream. In it I was standing in my bedroom with the gun. That was followed by the two new scenes from my tapestry: fighting with the man on my porch, and being shot. I added my thoughts to each image. The story was complete.

I was finishing when Ankou pulled aside the cloth. He looked around the room as if searching for some unseen object.

"Let's go."

I put the notebook and pencil in my bag and slipped it over my head so it sat on the hip opposite the dagger. He took my hand and led me out of the hut and across the plaza. Aurora and Sigrún watched as we turned onto the roadway leading to The Baron's palace.

We walked straight through the palace to the end of the long, desolate corridor. The door opened onto a large, ornate audience room. Like the smaller room where we met The Baron before, plush rugs were scattered around. Tapestries covered the walls. I hadn't noticed earlier, but every one was incomplete. Pulled out knots hung along bottom edges leaving them unfinished and ragged looking. I had a flash of righteous anger when I realized The Baron decorated this room with other people's tapestries.

Before I wondered if the rugs came from the workshop, we were standing in front of an empty throne raised several steps above the main level of the floor. Ankou pushed me and I knew to fall to my knees and touch my head to the ground. Ankou's foot on the back of my neck felt firm but not painful.

The most significant difference between this audience room and the smaller room was the stunning guide with his foot on the neck of another person. He was the angel who had taken the young man from the workshop. That man intrigued me. Except for my time at the loom, I had not been in the presence of someone like myself — someone dressed in the white clothing of the dead. I could not identify the person under the angel's foot. Was it was the weeping man?

Everyone remained silent and unmoving. I heard the sounds of another person in the room and smelled the faint sweet musk I associated with The Baron. Ankou removed his foot from my neck and I raised my head before he pulled on my hair.

The Baron lounged on the oversized throne, his legs splayed open before us. Where before he had acted cold, almost merciless, now he seemed friendly but arrogant. When I smiled he rewarded me with a conspiratorial wink. Did he also feel the draw between us?

I slid my eyes toward the person kneeling beside me. I was right. It was the young man I met in the workshop. Like me, he wore a tunic and trousers as well as leather arm guards. The weapon at his waist resembled my dagger. I couldn't see if he had a tapestry bag with a notebook hidden inside, but I assumed he did.

Before I could move, The Baron spoke. "Sam, Sara, you have done all you can here. Now I have a task for you." He smiled and again I felt that fluttering in my belly. "What a lovely couple," he said in a softer tone, almost as an aside.

"Stand up and look at each other."

I stood up and turned toward the man. I'm sure Sam wasn't his name any more than Sara was mine. He appeared to be in his late twenties with a well-formed body. His clear brown eyes held no evidence of his former weeping. He didn't appear to be anyone special and didn't excite my interest.

The Baron stepped down from his throne and stood in front of us. My heart beat faster as his musky odor enveloped us. Would he release me from this awful place?

He held out an elaborately carved but oddly shaped box with an ornate lock on one of the long sides. It was six-inch long coffin, wider where a body's shoulders would be, narrower where the head and feet belong.

"Hold out your hands." When we did, he set the box on them.

"My sister, Kore, who has styled herself the Queen of the Underworld, has asked that I return this trinket. You will be my emissaries. You must give this box to her, no one else. Do you understand?"

My dreams of staying here as The Baron's lover slipped. Sam and I nodded.

"I can see that your guides have prepared you for this journey, so you are ready to leave." The Baron paused, looking us over as if judging our fitness. "If you learn to work together, you'll survive. Otherwise..." He held his hands up and shrugged in an elaborate gesture. "Otherwise, well, you'll never leave the forests of the Nether Realm." His sinister smile sent a shiver of fear up my back. How could I ever have considered him as appealing?

He turned away and then looked back toward us. "The trinket inside is none of your concern. If you know what's good for you, you will not, I repeat, will not, open my little casket."

With that he turned again and disappeared behind the throne. I almost dropped the box. What had he given us? Before I could consider The Baron's words, Sam pulled the box away and tucked it into the bag at his side. My anger flared. He had taken The Baron's gift from me. Then I was relieved. Let him have the nasty thing.

"Come." Ankou grabbed my hand and pulled me toward a small opening between two tapestries on the wall. Sam and his guide followed. Ankou touched a spot behind one of the tapestries. A doorway swung open. As soon as we stepped into the garden beyond, the door swung shut and disappeared into the foreboding stone wall.

Ankou led us through the garden to a doorway in another wall. This door of smooth wood had no apparent hinges, handle, or lock. The words "Remember, Release, Return" and a wolf in full attack posture, eyes wide and teeth bared, marred its surface. The wolf looked familiar. When I first arrived, I had seen it on the sign pointing into the sinister forest. I remembered that dismal forest's subtle draw and my relief when Aurora led me away from it. Now I wanted to run through The Baron's palace, find him and tell him I couldn't do this. Ankou maintained his firm grip.

"Outside is the Nether Realm," the golden warrior said. "Once you step through this doorway, you cannot return but must follow the path through the forest and up the mountain to Kore's Temple. Give her The Baron's box. On your way you must remember and then release your previous lives. When you are successful, Kore, the Queen of the Dead, will lead you to the next phase of your journey."

"Do not linger or leave this path," Ankou added. "There are many hazards in the forest, many challenges before you approach the Temple. However, between the two of you, you have what you need."

He touched a spot on the wall and the door swung inward. Ankou squeezed my hand and then pushed me through the opening. Sam followed and I heard the door slam shut. We stood in the place The Baron called the Nether Realm.

CHAPTER 12

We had stepped from full sunlight into an eerie half-lit dusk. Giant trees, bushes and brambles formed a barrier that defined a path leading away from where we stood. The dirt was worn smooth as though trampled by a thousand feet. Colorless gray surrounded us: the trees, the brambles on either side of the path, the path itself. I had first seen this forest and the image of the wolf when Aurora and I stopped at the crossroads. I had thought myself lucky to gain the light and beauty of Empyrean. Now my luck had changed. I was condemned to the land of the hungry wolf, the Nether Realm.

I started walking and then remembered my companion. The man still stood by the door. When I went to him and touched his arm, he shivered. There was no wind, but my own thin tunic and trousers felt insubstantial against the predators I felt were surrounding us. Fear raced up my back and settled between my shoulder blades. The man stared at me, his brown eyes wide, furrows forming on his forehead. He seemed even more shocked than I was.

"They call me Sara." I smiled at him. If we were to be partners, I wanted to start out right. "But I'm sure that's not my real name."

The man nodded.

"I assume Sam isn't your name either."

He nodded again.

"Do you know your name?"

He shook his head.

"We can't go back." I waved at the door, sitting flush with the wall with no visible hardware. "All we can do is go forward and hope for the best. Come on."

"I'm not supposed to be here," he whimpered. "I wasn't supposed to die."

"None of us were supposed to die." I snapped. Did he think I was happy with these circumstances? "But here we are, ejected from the *pleasures* of the Empyrean." My voice rose, hoping Ankou heard my anger on the other side of the wall.

My so-called companion stood as if rooted, tears streaming down his face. I felt rather than heard the swoosh of wings, followed by a high-pitched cry when the owl caught its prey. Sam shivered again. Would he stay here, hoping for re-entry into the palace? Good. Whatever hazards and challenges awaited, I would do better on my own, without the weight of his sorrow holding me back.

"Give me the box." I held out my hand. "You can stay here if you want, but I'm going to go find this Queen of the Dead. I have a few questions for her."

"I can't." He wiped away his tears and looked into the forest. With another shiver he seemed to decide. "I have to go with you. We're compeers. Didn't you hear The Baron? We won't make it if we don't stick together."

He was right. Much as I hated the idea, I was stuck with this sniveling loser. I took his hand and tugged. "Then come along." He resisted at first and then took a step forward. I'm not sure what happened, but between his resistance and his step his posture changed. He wiped his eyes and stood straighter. A new confidence appeared to animate him.

I pulled him along behind me. The path turned and widened so we could walk side by side. Still holding my hand, Sam adjusted his strides to mine. Perhaps he would be a useful companion after all.

Now that we were moving, I looked around, gauging our new situation. When the door first shut behind us, the woods were silent, as though no life survived in this desolate place. Now I heard small animal noises, birds calling and flying from tree to tree, something moving through the underbrush. In the distance, coyotes yelped and sang of a successful hunt. I heard other noises, too. It reminded me of the soundtrack of a badly made horror film. I almost expected a creepy undertone of organ music.

When I looked at Sam, he raised his eyebrows.

"I don't know," I said, responding to his silent question. I loosened my dagger in its scabbard. When Sigrún trained me, she must have been preparing me for this Nether Realm. "Maybe if we keep moving everything will be all right."

Of course, hoping for an easy journey was futile. As we rounded another curve, an enormous wolf blocked our way. It bared its teeth and growled. I'd forgotten the rule. When you met a menacing wolf, did you make yourself big and intimidating or small and harmless-looking?

Sam pulled me into a squat that put us eye level with the creature. I slipped my dagger out of its scabbard. The weight reassured me. The animal continued to stare, growling.

"Don't make eye contact with him," Sam whispered. "That's a challenge to any wild animal."

I lowered my head but kept the animal in my peripheral vision. The growling stopped. Sam held out his hand, as you would with a new dog, palm up, fingers loose. The wolf looked from him to me, then back to him again. It took a step forward, stopped, and sat in the middle of the road, growling again.

"That's it, boy." Sam's voice was calm. "We're harmless."

The wolf stood and trotted toward us, stopping just beyond Sam's fingers. I tense, prepared to leap at it. A thrust from underneath would be most effective, but that would put me at the mercy of its teeth and claws. I'd have to attack from the top. Was my dagger long enough to find the wolf's heart?

As I waited for the creature to decide what to do, I wondered whether it could be killed or was it dead like us? What would happen if it attacked? If it mauled us? Would we heal or stay torn to pieces? I didn't want to find out. Perhaps Sam was right to befriend it.

"Come on, boy," Sam said, his voice quiet, soothing. "Come on. See, we're friends. We won't hurt you."

The wolf took another step and sniffed Sam's out-stretched fingers. Then it licked them. Sam reached forward and buried both hands in the animal's fur, scratching and ruffling it. After a moment, it sat again. I slipped my dagger back into its scabbard.

"Hold your hand out like I did," Sam said in that calm voice. "Let him smell you, too."

I extended my left hand, aware again of its sharp teeth. It sniffed at me, licked my fingers, and then looked at me with his amber-colored eyes. I felt an understanding passed between us.

"Good boy." Sam dug his fingers deeper into its coat. He stood, his hands still embedded in the ruff of fur around the wolf's neck. I rose with him, keeping my motion smooth and non-threatening.

"Now," he said, "tell your friends to let us pass."

I looked beyond our wolf and saw more wolves than I could count, watching us from the path. My bravado sank deep into my stomach. I might have been able to fight off a single animal, but I would have lost against an entire pack.

In a single motion, they glided into the trees and disappeared, although I imagined I could still see their eyes watching. Only our wolf remained, Sam's hands still caught in its fur.

He loosened his grip on the animal, and we took a cautious step forward. It moved forward too. Then it took a few steps up the trail, stopped, turned around, and sat again. It looked back as if to say, Well, aren't you coming?

We walked forward. The wolf waited until we had almost caught up to him. Then he trotted off, staying several paces in front of us.

Sam laughed. "It looks like we have an escort."

"And not only your new friend." I peered into the underbrush. "The rest are still there, watching."

He laughed again. "Of course they are. I think the pack's adopted us."

Only when we started walking did I realize my heart was hammering a wild rhythm of fear and anticipation. I had been prepared to defend myself but Sam had remained calm and defused the situation. We had not only gained a companion but a whole pack of protectors.

"Who are you?" I demanded after we had walked for a while.

"I can't remember… anything." His voice caught. Would he start crying again? But he pulled himself up straighter. "That's not true. I died in a hospital hooked up to a thousand different machines. I left behind a young wife and several small children." He shook his head. "I shouldn't have died like that."

"Aurora, my guide, told me I needed to remember." I wanted to share what I had discovered with this stranger. "But all I got from that horrid loom was that I was murdered by someone trying to break into my home. Aurora implied that I had been a bad person, but…" I paused. "At first I thought I was in heaven, but Empyrean isn't how I expected heaven to be. And now we've been kicked out of there and landed in this…" I waved at the surrounding desolation.

We walked side-by-side for a while.

"Do you always jump straight to attack mode when threatened?" Sam asked as we followed the wolf.

"What do you mean?" I hissed. I knew what he was asking, but I wanted to hear him accuse me of having almost gotten us killed back there.

"The first thing you did when you saw our wolf friend here was pull out your dagger. Is that the way you always react?" His voice sounded dispassionate, not judgmental.

There was a long silence while I considered Sam's question. His accusation seemed plausible, and I considered what I knew about myself. When I thought someone was breaking into my house, I pulled a gun out of my nightstand. I took action. Even when I didn't know what was happening.

From the moment I stepped off that boat, I had fought first with Aurora and then with Sigrún. I hadn't been a willing or passive student. Instead I had always questioned the things Aurora wanted me to do. I hated her, and I hated that detestable loom. Sigrún, the Valkyrie, repelled me from the first time she came into my hut. I had feared her, but I also reveled in the time I spent with her in the arena. Knowing how to defend myself, and how to take the offensive, felt important. I relished the fight.

Ever since I landed here, I had resisted being controlled and was willing to argue with people who had much more power than I did. I put up a tough front, even when I was afraid.

"Yes," I admitted.

"Yes what?" .

"Yes, I think I'm willing to defend myself—no matter what." I looked at him. "But you didn't assume that we would have to defend ourselves against the wolf. Why is that? Why weren't you afraid?"

Now it was Sam's turn to be quiet.

"I don't know. I didn't think about it. I was afraid, but somehow that wolf looked familiar. Maybe I had a dog like that once… before." He shook his head as though he found his own thoughts unbelievable.

We kept walking.

"We're already dead, so what could a single animal do? You'd already pulled your dagger, so I guess I expected you would defend us if things went bad." He paused. "No, that's not right. I didn't think of all that. I should have been more afraid, but making friends seemed like a good idea."

After another long pause, he continued, "Now I can see all the ways it could have gone wrong. Thank you for being prepared if my hunch hadn't played out."

The wolf that had been trotting along ahead stopped and sat facing us, keeping us from continuing.

CHAPTER 13

We stopped. Everything appeared the same, except for the wolf who sat facing us, ears alert, in the middle of the trail. The forest noises had stilled.

Again, I drew my dagger and held it against my leg. Sam did the same. Now we both were ready to take action. We stepped closer together, standing side-by-side.

Neither of us moved. Nor did the wolf.

After a moment, it growled. A small, dirty-white rabbit raced out of the woods and froze on the trail between the wolf and us. It was close enough for us to see its little nose twitching. Before we could react, a grayish-brown owl swooped down, grabbed it and flew away with it.

The wolf yelped once, then raced to where the rabbit had been as though intent on recovering what had been stolen from him.

Sam and I looked at each other. What had just happened? I shook my head, replacing my weapon into its scabbard.

After following the rabbit's trail into the underbrush and finding nothing, the wolf returned to sit at our feet.

"Good boy." Sam ruffed its fur. I did the same and allowed it to lick my cupped hands. As he turned and trotted up the trail, we heard a mournful, mewing scream from the direction the owl had taken. Like me, Sam shivered.

The sounds of the forest returned. A soft breeze slipped through the underbrush, playing a counterpoint to the small animal sounds and birdcalls. Our passage made no sound on the well-worn path. We walked, lost in our own thoughts.

Had the rabbit been as surprised at its death as I had been with mine? I did not know my whole story, but it appeared I was living a good life when a stranger's visit ended everything for me. Who attacked me? What happened to him after I died? Had he escaped or was he rotting in a jail somewhere, even looking into the face of his own death? A vindictive part of me hoped he had been caught, tried, and was awaiting execution.

But that was the past. Now I needed to learn more about this compeer I had been given. I turned to him. "Didn't we meet at the pavilion?"

He nodded, and I wondered if I had provoked another surge of tears.

"You have a stunning guardian." I attempted a more neutral topic than our deaths.

"Michael." He nodded. "He was helping me, helping me remember... remember who I was... before."

I heard the catch in his voice, his difficulty talking about his life.

"My guardians wanted me to remember, too." I grimaced. But they weren't very helpful. Would my time in the Empyrean have been more pleasant if I had had more sympathetic guardians? I would have traded all three of them for the gorgeous Michael.

"I didn't learn much, though," I confided, wary of exposing myself.

He shook his head. "It was a horrid mistake. I should never..."

We lapsed into silence.

"We're here now." I sighed. "Wherever 'here' is. Maybe if we make it to Kore's Temple and deliver The Baron's box, we'll get answers."

I glanced at the man The Baron called my compeer. He was still the picture of hopelessness. Shoulders slumped, feet dragging, more tears sliding down his face. However long this trip took, it would be unpleasant with this dispirited companion.

When I glanced away from him and up the trail, I saw the wolf had stopped again. As we approached, he growled a warning. Once again I pulled out my dagger. Sam did the same. I slipped behind him so we were back-to-back. Between us we had a complete three hundred and sixty degree view of our surroundings. But again there was nothing to see. We waited. The stillness was different this time. It felt more sinister.

As sudden as a clap of thunder, a huge brown body burst from the forest. At first, I thought it was a deer. Then I realized it was a man wearing antlers and a loose leather cloak. A second person followed him. This one wore the skin of a tawny feline. They disappeared into the forest and then emerged again in front of me. The two stood in the center of the trail, panting as though they had run a long way. The cat-man carried a pointed stick as tall as himself. He used it to poke the deer-man who ran to where we stood mesmerized. The deer-man grabbed Sam's wrist and pulled him up the road. The cat-man chased them, letting out an inhuman scream of triumph. They disappeared around a bend further up the path.

Before I could take a breath, more people, all dressed like the cat-man, came from the trees. I stood stunned as they flowed around me like I was a rock in the middle of a river. They raced after Sam and his abductors.

"Sara-a-a-a." Sam's voice echoed through the woods. Then it fell silent.

As the last of the crowd rounded the bend in the trail, I continued to stare toward where my compeer had disappeared, leaving me alone, abandoned, with only the wolf for company.

CHAPTER 14

The wolf stood, gave a yelp to gain my attention, and followed the crowd of cat-men. Shaking myself from my momentary daze, I jogged up the path until I caught up to the wolf, waiting for me around the next bend. I wanted to fall to my knees and bury my face in his fur as I imagined Sam would do. Instead, I reached into the dirt to pick up Sam's dagger. He must have dropped it as the deer-man dragged him away.

Still grasping my own dagger, I slid Sam's into my sheath, and then stood with my hand on the wolf's head. My stoic facade cracked. Shivers of fear ran through my body. The noises of the forest returned as though nothing unusual had happened, but Sam was gone, taken by… by what? I did not know what I was up against, but I knew I had to rescue my compeer. I couldn't face this dark and dangerous place alone.

The wolf slipped from beneath my hand and trotted up the path. After a moment he stopped, sat and barked, calling me to follow him.

I shook away the fear that paralyzed me and ran after my new companion whom I named Wolf in my mind. The whole pack of wolves that must have been watching from behind the trees rushed to surround me. The deer-man who had taken Sam had his horde of cat-people, but I had Wolf and his pack. We may have evened up the odds for whatever would confront us.

Wolf ran with his nose to the ground, following the scent of Sam's kidnappers around the next bend in the trail, then another, and another. Then the terrain changed. I hadn't noticed the incline until I challenged this body to keep up with Wolf and his pack. I was panting when the trees thinned out. The path became steeper and rockier, no longer soft dirt. Without thinking, I ran after Wolf, the peach pit pricking my chest with each step. When he veered into the woods on our right, I didn't stop to consider the implications. Instead, I followed him, surrounded by the loping pack.

I expected the plants to be winter-dead, cold and brittle. They weren't. Everything was shades of gray and black, but the touch of the trees and bushes was that of living underbrush, not soft but pliable. I ran through the forest, unmindful of the sticks and rocks beneath my feet, following Wolf. We were far from the path when he stopped short of a clearing. I squatted next to him, and surrounded by the pack, surveyed the scene in front of us.

The woods gave way to a meadow of gray, knee-high grasses. I could see the deer-man with the cat-people gathered in a circle around him. At first I could not find Sam. Then I realized he stood in the center of the group as one of the cat-people danced around him, jabbing at him with his pointed stick. It looked as though Sam was trying to stay out of the reach of the man's weapon.

Sam panted as he tried to parry the blows with his arm. The sounds of jeers and taunting of the cat-people filled the meadow as they cheered on their leader. How long before the cat-man landed a serious blow?

Wolf growled and his pack answered. They wanted to attack, but I hesitated, remembering Sam's question when we'd first met Wolf. Attacking then would have been disastrous, but now I did not see any other choice. Not wanting to be impetuous, I continued to watch.

It looked as though only the leader of the cat-men had a weapon. The rest would be no match for the wolf pack. I was still holding my dagger in my right hand. With my left, I reached across my body and pulled Sam's dagger out of my scabbard. Jumping up, I screamed and raced toward them, teeth bared and a dagger in each hand. Wolf ran at my side with his howling pack close behind.

The crowd scattered, leaving their leader and Sam alone in the meadow. While the pack followed the escaping cat-men into the forest, I stepped between my compeer and his adversary, moving into one of the fighting poses Sigrún taught me.

My opponent wore a dirty white tunic and trousers, covered by what looked like the skin of some big cat. I wondered if he could injure or even kill me. When I fought the Valkyrie she had caused no real damage. Instead she left me sore and bruised. But I did not know whether that was because I couldn't be seriously wounded or because Sigrún wasn't trying to hurt me.

"Who dares to come here?" he shouted, jabbing his spear toward me. "This man is mine."

Instead of responding, I parried his thrusts, circling around, forcing him to follow my movements. I realized he did not have Sigrún's training. His weapon was not as dangerous as her sword. The spear only had one small cutting edge on its tip. If I could evade that point, I could reach the man himself.

I feinted a couple of times, coming at him under his weapon but never getting close enough to touch him. I backed up, forcing him to thrust farther from his body, which threw him off balance. I dropped Sam's dagger, grabbed the spear, twisted it out of the man's hand and threw it away. Then I lunged, thrusting my own dagger under his chin. A tiny drop of blood colored his grimy neck. When he tried to step back, a menacing growl alerted him to Wolf's presence behind him.

He raised his arms in the universal sign of defeat. When I pulled my dagger away, he squatted, keeping his empty hands splayed out in front of him.

CHAPTER 15

Up close, the cat-man looked young, like a teenager who had not yet lost all his baby fat or taken up shaving. His tunic and trousers had once been white but now they were filthy. His hair hung in greasy strings around his head. He should have been afraid of me but instead he seemed at ease and in control.

After a moment he smiled. "Welcome, fierce Sara," he said as though he were the winner of our struggle. "Welcome to the tribe of the Stone Cold Panthers." He continued to hold his open hands in front of him.

Sam came from behind me to stand at my side. Picking up his dagger, he wiped the blade on the leg of his trousers and slipped it into its sheath. He looked at the man sitting on his haunches for a moment and then walked around him and greeted Wolf. "Good boy." He ruffed Wolf's fur. "I see you called out the troops."

I crouched to be at eye-level with my opponent. I continued to stare at him, daring him to make a move against us.

"Who are you people?" I intended to scream but my voice was low. Those few words contained all my anger and fear.

"You two were on your way to the Temple," the cat-man said as if we had forgotten. "Me and my band, we were on that journey, too. But we've taken a detour." He laughed at some private joke. "Do you know you're on a one-way trip?"

I lowered my dagger. Sam stepped to my left side and squatted beside me. He slid his hand down my arm and enfolded my hand in his. Wolf left his post to join us, sitting on my right.

"Many others have come through these woods, traveling to the Temple, but no one has ever come back. Who knows what happens up there?" The cat-man nodded his head toward what I assumed was the general direction of Kore's Temple. He shivered. "Everyone finishes that journey, eventually. But in the meantime, me and the other Stone Cold Panthers... well, we're free. As free as anyone can be in what they call the Nether Realm."

He paused, as if listening to the sounds of the forest. "There are many dangers here. Not only wild animals," he nodded toward Wolf, "but other gangs, too. My people stick together. Help each other out. We're a family."

He unfolded himself to stand. Raising my dagger again, I pulled Sam up with me. I continued to watch this ruffian who stood before us, unfazed by my weapon or the fact I had already beaten him once.

He looked from me to Sam and back. The grin that spread over his face was warm, playful. "Will you two join us?" He looked at me. "The Stone Cold Panthers would welcome your fierce power, Sara."

I tried to understand what he was saying. Was he inviting us to abandon our journey and join his roving band of cat-men? Before I could think about what that might mean, I barked out a laugh at the absurdity of it all. We weren't ragamuffins like his little gang. We were on a mission for The Baron, after all.

He turned. Ignoring his spear he walked to the deer-man's cloak abandoned in the grass. Returning to us, he bowed and held it out to me. I looked at Sam. What was this?

"Take it," the boy said, "you are a worthy opponent."

I touched the cloak. It was soft and warm. I realized how few gentle things I had found since I woke up on that boat. I slipped my dagger back into its sheath, took the cloak and dropped it over my shoulders. It felt like love, warming me to my depths.

"Thank you." I smiled. He returned my smile, his dark eyes twinkling. Without another word, he picked up his spear and walked away, leaving Sam, Wolf, and me alone in the center of the meadow.

"What just happened?" I asked Sam.

"I don't know." He stood silent for a long time. "Thank you for bringing the wolf and his pack." He stared toward the forest that surrounded us. "I don't know what I would have done otherwise."

I had followed Sam and his abductors without thinking about what might happen. Standing on that path with only Wolf for a companion, I had felt I must rescue Sam, regardless of the consequences. I could not endure being alone in this dismal place. For all my willingness to fight and my training with Sigrún, I realized in that moment that inside I was just a little girl afraid of the dark.

I squeezed Sam's hand. "We're compeers," I said, unwilling to share my fears with this man who was still almost a stranger. "We have to stick together."

Without further discussion, we sank to the ground. I was physically and emotionally drained by my mad dash through the forest, my skirmish with the cat-man, and its aftermath. Sam probably felt the same.

When I felt like myself again, I looked around. The leader of the Stone Cold Panthers had left us far from the route we were taking to Kore's Temple.

"Do you have any idea where we are or how to get back to the path?" I asked, afraid of the answer.

Horror passed over Sam's face. He shook his head. We were truly and completely lost.

CHAPTER 16

I looked around. I thought I knew where Wolf and I had waited with the pack watching Sam's fight. Now I wasn't sure. I saw no distinguishing landmarks, not even the mountain where the so-called Queen of the Dead was supposed to be waiting for us. The dismal forest surrounded us and no one direction appeared more promising than another. The cat-man and his Tribe of the Stone Cold Panthers had scattered. They had not even left a path through the grass.

"We're lost." Sam collapsed to the ground and cradled his head in his hands. Soft, desolate moans escaped between his fingers. Wolf sat next to him, whimpering, and trying to lick his face.

The sky was gray and featureless. I could not see into the surrounding forest more than a foot or two in any direction. Even if I found where I had rushed into this meadow, had I left enough of a trail to find our way back to the path? I didn't think so.

I put my arm around Sam's shoulders. What else could I do? Wolf alternated licking my hand and Sam's face. The exhilaration I had felt in defeating the cat-man and the pleasure of the deer-man's cloak drained away, leaving me exhausted.

As my miserable compeer whimpered beside me, I tried to remember what Ankou said when we left The Baron's palace. He said not to leave the path. Well, it was too late to change that. What else had he said? He had warned of challenges and hazards along the way. Until we realized we were lost, I thought we had done well on that score. I replayed our final moments in the Empyrean in my head and found an important hint. He had said between us we had everything we needed.

I pulled off the leather cloak and spread it on the ground. "Dump out your bag." I reached to remove my own bag.

He raised his head and looked at me.

"Did they give you a map?" I said. "Ankou said we have what we need. Let's see what we've got."

I did not have much: my notebook and pencil, and a coin. One side had an image of an open-air Greek-style temple complete with colonnades. I thought of the Parthenon. On the other was the same attacking wolf carved on the door between The Baron's Palace and the Nether Realm. I wondered if we would have to buy our way into Kore's Temple. Would one small coin be enough?

I flipped through my notebook to see if any new pages had appeared. Nothing.

Sam watched for a moment and then wiped his eyes. He pulled off his own bag and spread its contents on the cloak. All he had was his notebook and pencil, and the box The Baron gave us to take to his sister. The notebook reminded me of the one I had seen back in my hut, the book that zapped me when I tried to pick it up. Sam's notebook had the same green triangles, red spiral, and blue waves as mine. Instead of the skull and crossed bones, his had a child-like skull with angel wings. I wondered about the different images.

Sam flipped through the notebook and then shook his head. "No map."

I looked at the two small piles spread out on the cloak. It wasn't much. I reached for the box, stopping my hand short of touching it. Would it shock me like Sam's notebook back in my hut?

"Go ahead," he said. "He gave it to both of us."

I tried to pick it up. It didn't zap me, but stuck to the ground.

"Well, maybe not." Sam picked up the box and held it with both hands with the same gesture The Baron used to give it to us.

Elaborate carvings covered all sides of the miniature coffin. The lid showed a stylized figure laid out asleep or dead, its arms crossed. It wore the same tunic and trousers as Sam and I. The figure was a skeleton with a leering skull and bony fingers and toes. Small red stones took the place of the eyes. Blooming vines with tiny birds and flowers surrounded it. On one side a golden latch held the lid closed. When I reached for the lock, Sam put his hand over mine.

"The Baron said not to open this."

I wanted to protest. What if this box held a map?

But The Baron had been specific. I set the box on top of Sam's bag. There was no map. In spite of Ankou's promise, we had nothing helpful.

I looked across the meadow. "Maybe Wolf's friends are watching, and they'll come and lead us back on the path." I tried to sound hopeful but failed.

Sam shook his head. Wolf seemed content to sit with us.

We were alone and lost. I wondered if we should have given up our quest and accepted the cat-man's offer. He and his gang seemed to know the forest of the Nether Realm. Perhaps if we had not rejected his offer, he would have led us back to the path. At least if we had joined the Stone Cold Panthers, we would be with other people like ourselves.

I shook my head. It had not been a mistake to follow Sam's abductors and rescue him. I could not have continued alone, without the box. As I stared at our meager collection, I heard the low, deep hooting of an owl.

CHAPTER 17

Sam continued to study the small pile spread out before us. Ignoring everything else, he picked up the box to look at it again. He bounced his arm up and down as though weighing it. "It feels alive like something inside is moving."

"Ick." I tried to image what could be in the tiny coffin. Maybe it was a good thing Sam had kept me from opening it and releasing whatever it contained. I thought about the myth of Pandora's box. In Greek mythology, Pandora was a delightful woman who was given many gifts, including a beautiful chest. She had been warned not to open it, but of course, she disobeyed. As a consequence, she released all the evil in the world. I had been told the story was a warning to nosy women.

Sam continued fiddling with our box, turning it this way and that. The golden clasp holding it shut was a simple affair—a metal loop with a tiny bolt. It would have been easy to remove the bolt, open it, and discover what was inside. I promised myself I would not make the same mistake Pandora had. Around the clasp I recognized the carvings as deer-man and his cat-men companions. When Sam turned the box I could see a pack similar to Wolf's family on the other long side.

Before I could wonder about the relationship between those images and the other dwellers of the Nether Realm we had met, Sam put the box on his open palm. The "head" pointed behind us and to the right. I reached out, then drew my hand back, and just looked at it. The casket was a macabre object, but I saw nothing else unusual about it.

"See what happens when I turn it." Sam lifted the box, turned it ninety degrees, and set it back on his palm.

At first nothing happened. Then the box turned until the head pointed back behind Sam. He picked it up again and set it down facing the opposite direction. We watched mesmerized as it rotated until it pointed toward the same spot in the trees.

"It's a compass of sorts." Sam picked up the box again, rotated it and set it down. "The question is what is it pointing to?" It turned again. "Is that the way to Kore's Temple or is it pointing north and the Temple is east?"

He turned the box several more times. Each time it moved itself until it pointed back to the same place. That was a nice trick, but it didn't seem useful without a map or something to tell us where we were.

"The Baron said this box belonged to his sister, the Queen of the Underworld." I tried to work out my thoughts. "Maybe, somehow, it knows where her temple is."

I looked behind us. The trees in that direction looked the same as any other part of the forest.

"Of course." Sam smiled for the first time since we had started on our journey. "The box must be pointing us toward Kore's Temple. That's the only thing that makes sense. We don't need a map. We don't even need the path. We just need to walk the way the box tells us." He shoved his notebook into his bag. "Come on, let's go."

I put my hand on his arm, stopping him. "What if I'm wrong? You said earlier, what if the box is pointing north and Kore's Temple is east? Or worse, what if it leads up back to The Baron's Palace?" We should not return to the Empyrean without completing our mission.

We sat still. I felt that Sam was right, but I was not yet willing to move forward on a mere conjecture. I did not want to make an impulsive decision that made our situation worse.

"You have to be right." Sam's words came slower as if he, too, considered our options. "If Ankou told us the truth and we have everything we need, then this," he waved his hand over our paltry collection, "has to be enough to get us where we need to go."

He paused. "Besides, what alternatives do we have? Sitting here isn't getting us closer to Kore's Temple. If we follow the box and we're wrong, we won't be any more lost than we are now." He reached out and ruffed Wolf's fur. "Let's do it."

Wolf yipped his agreement as I continued to consider what Sam had said. My compeer was right. We were not getting closer to our destination, and this was the best idea either of us had had. I gathered up my notebook and the coin and put them back into my bag. Then I picked up my cloak and scrambled to my feet.

Sam put the coffin on his palm, turning himself until it pointed straight ahead. He grabbed my hand, and we took a step forward. The box held steady as we approached the forest.

I took a deep breath. *I hope this works.*

CHAPTER 18

I expected to find Wolf's pack waiting for us when we walked into the forest, but I was wrong. Instead, it was desolate and gray, lonely and foreboding. Sam dropped my hand when we left the meadow. Since there was no path, we couldn't walk side-by-side. My stomach twisted when I stepped behind him. I should be in front, but he was the one with the box. He needed to go first. So it was Sam, then me, then Wolf. When I realized that being in the middle protected me, it calmed my annoyance at following someone else.

Sam found the easiest way through the undergrowth while still keeping us headed in the general direction the box pointed. I thought my cloak would catch on the tree limbs and bushes. Instead, the leather let everything slide across its surface, protecting my arms and legs from being scratched. It wasn't cold in the forest of the Nether Realm but the cloak was warm and comforting. I wondered why the deer-man abandoned it. Maybe he intended to return later. Perhaps we should have left it, but the cat-man had offered it as my reward for winning our battle, and I took it.

Although we had been walking on a slight incline since leaving the meadow, soon the way became steeper. That was a sign that we were headed up the mountain toward what The Baron called Kore's Temple.

As we continued, I considered the young man in front of me. The guides referred to him as my compeer, but I didn't really know what that meant. He had been a good companion so far. He kept us from being attacked by Wolf and his pack. He recognized the compass-like characteristic of the Queen of the Underworld's box. Now he was leading our little group through this endless forest.

We had been thrown together at random, with no connection until we met at The Baron's palace. I still didn't understand why I raced after him when he was abducted. More than my fear of the dark made me willing to fight the cat-man to save him.

It wasn't his looks. Like all the people in the workshop back in Empyrean, his features were ordinary, making him neither extremely appealing nor extraordinarily unappealing. He was well built, without the pronounced muscles of an athlete but not flabby like someone too lazy to exercise.

Following him, I realized Sam was attractive as a human being. He still had feelings for the family he left behind by dying. I had no memory of anyone except the vague figure of my attacker. There was also the way he approached Wolf. I would have let my fear lead us into a battle of daggers against teeth and claws — a battle we would have lost. Even though Wolf appeared menacing, Sam assumed he wouldn't hurt us. As a consequence we gained a companion. If Sam hadn't befriended Wolf, how would I ever have followed the cat-men through the forest? My stomach clenched at the thought I might have been left alone in the middle of that path.

I wasn't as good a compeer to Sam as he had been to me. Sam didn't need me. At every point, he had been the one to make the right decision or figure out the puzzle. If I hadn't shown up, he would have made some accommodation with the cat-man and his people. If I disappeared, he and Wolf would be able to carry out The Baron's charge without me. My stomach twisted at the thought of being alone here in the Nether Realm. Sam didn't need me, but I was terrified of continuing without him.

We reached the top of one ridge. Although there was still an upward tilt, the path became less steep, and the forest retreated. We weren't in a meadow, but the bushes and brambles thinned out. Sam picked up his pace, and soon we were jogging side-by-side with Wolf trotting along, his tongue lolling out of his open mouth.

In spite of the peach pit sending a tingle of irritation through me with each step, I was astonished at the ease with which this body could continue. I drew my thoughts away from Sam and back to my situation. Aurora said there was more I needed to learn about my death, so I let my mind drift, hoping that some insight would occur to me.

I am sitting at an over-sized desk in a corner office in a large city. Behind me, floor-to-ceiling windows show a sprawling metropolis. In front of me sits a young man with straight black hair, quick dark eyes, and swarthy skin. I am interviewing him, and by his slight accent I know he is Hispanic. His resume, work samples, and the evaluations of my staff and others are spread in front of me. He is extraordinary. The son of an immigrant family, he is the first to have attended college. According to the reports I've read, he excelled in the coding I needed to take my company to the next level.

I won't hire him. Employee benefits are too expensive. We'll take him on as a contractor. He smiles when I make him a low-ball offer, salary only, no benefits, the possibility of stock options later. He is one of the brightest young people of his generation, but he hasn't yet learned the ways of business. He doesn't realize he is worth twice what I am offering. I will be getting a great deal on him. After walking around the wide expanse of my desk and shaking his hand, I escort him to the door.

"Marsha," I say to the woman waiting on the other side. "Show Juan around. He'll be starting Monday."

I close the door as the two of them walk away. Getting Juan Garcia was a coup. I know my competitors would love to have him. If everything works out, and he proves to be as good as he appeared, maybe I'd promote him to my executive board someday. We would make a good team.

I look at the city spread out at my feet. In six months, the world will learn about the work of Juan and the rest of my staff. I will take the company public, repaying my early investors and justifying my expansive salary. The Wired Entrepreneur will probably do a lead story about me. I am one smart cookie.

Before I could react to this new revelation about my past, I almost bumped into Sam who had stopped running. We are standing on the edge of a deep canyon. In the open now, we saw Kore's Temple in the distance. Its white walls shone like a beacon above the dark desolate forest. We didn't need the box to show us where to go, but we couldn't continue. The abyss in front of us was an impassable barrier in both directions as far as we could see.

The three of us stood panting, looking across the canyon at the temple, and up and down its length. Sam picked up the box and pointed it first one way and then the other. Both times it rotated to point toward the temple, apparently unaware of the barrier in front of us. Great black birds circled down into the gorge, riding the air.

"We'll have to go around" I was not embarrassed to state the obvious. "The question is, which direction?"

Sam shook his head, unwilling to choose. I fingered the peach pit at the top of my cleavage and wondered what the person in my vision would do. It appeared that I had been a rich and successful businesswoman. I must have been decisive, but now I didn't have enough information. *Well then, we'll have to take a chance.*

I dug into my bag and pulled out the coin. One side showed the image of Kore's Temple. The other side was a portrait of Wolf in full attack posture, eyes flashing and teeth bared. It didn't matter which side was heads and which tails.

I showed the coin to Sam. "Temple we go right. Wolf left."

Sam nodded, and I flipped the coin. It spun around several times, then fell Wolf-side up. Left seemed as good as right. I looked at Sam and he nodded again. Left it was.

I picked up the coin and dropped it back into my bag. Sam slipped the box back into his. We could see where we needed to go, even if we couldn't get there.

Turning, we walk along the edge of the canyon. I hoped we'd made the correct choice.

CHAPTER 19

Wolf sat on the edge of the canyon, refusing to follow us. Did he know something we didn't? Should we have gone the other way? There was no incline. We couldn't see which way the water flowed at the bottom of the canyon. We had no way of knowing if we had made a mistake. As we were about to lose sight of Wolf, Sam turned and whistled.

"Wolf. Come on, boy." He clapped his hands, but the wolf refused to budge.

"Should we have gone the other way?" He looked at me. "Do you want to turn back?"

I shrugged. One way was as good as the other. We looked toward our companion, silhouetted against the gray sky. He looked so forlorn, abandoned.

I glanced from Wolf, to Kore's Temple across the ravine, to Sam. Did it make a difference, which way we went? I had not made many decisions in my afterlife. Why should I let this one depend on the fall of a coin? I thought about the woman I used to be. She didn't hesitate. I had not been some loser, but a successful businesswoman. Sam had led us through the forest. Now it was my turn to take charge.

"Come on." I grabbed Sam's hand and pulled him back toward where Wolf sat waiting. "Let's go back."

Wolf watched us retrace our steps, dancing around like a puppy. Unable to control himself, he trotted toward us. Sam let go of my hand and ran to meet him, burying his face in Wolf's ruff. I slowed my walk, giving Sam time. When Sam released him, Wolf trotted to me and sat. I buried my hands in his fur. He licked my face as if welcoming me back. I smiled when I realized this was the first time since I came to this place that someone, or something, acted happy to see me.

When I stood up, Sam looked at me. "Are you sure?" His concern was obvious.

I shook my head. I did not know which was the right direction but if Wolf wanted us to go right, then there was no reason to argue. Perhaps the coin had told us to defer to Wolf.

"No," I said, "but maybe Wolf knows something we don't."

The edge of the canyon was rocky with little vegetation. After a while, Sam picked up the pace and soon the three of us were jogging side-by-side. Kore's Temple was so close, glowing as though it had an inner light. As we jogged, I wondered if we could jump across the canyon. It was too wide for any normal human being to hurdle, but then, we weren't normal human beings. We couldn't die — we were already dead — but what if we fell into this canyon? Perhaps if we could see the bottom of it, we'd discover that it was filled with the bones of others who had tried to cross.

Nothing seemed to change. It felt as though we were jogging in place. On our right, the dark, desolate forest. Across the canyon, Kore's Temple. This edge of the canyon fluctuated back and forth. Sometimes we were closer to the temple, sometimes farther away, but always the abyss remained.

I remembered my vision. It confirmed my earlier suspicion. I had been an important person and clever. I had gotten people like Juan to work for me, even at an absurd salary.

"Do you remember anything of your life, before?" I asked Sam as we loped along. "Do you remember how you died?"

"I was shot by the police." He spoke without emotion. "My family kept me alive for a while. If I recovered, I could clear my name. But I was hurt too bad. They had to let me go."

"I was shot, too," I told him. "But I'm not sure how it happened. I thought I had it figured out, back at the workshop. Aurora said I would learn more out here in the Nether Realm, but I don't see how."

Sam stopped, panting. "Maybe the Queen of the Dead can tell us. Maybe she'll be so happy to get her box back she'll... she'll... I don't know." He looked toward the Temple. "Do you think she might let us go back?"

Shaking my head, I jogged in place. I wanted to keep moving. I'd lost any sense of time since I woke up on that boat, but assuming we had died before we arrived here, we had probably already had funerals and been buried. Perhaps we'd been dead for a long time, months, years even.

"I don't think we can go back." I looked over at Sam. Tears crept from his eyes and slid down his face.

Slipping my arm around his shoulder, I gave him an awkward squeeze. "I'm sorry. You must have loved them very much."

He nodded. "When I close my eyes, I can see their faces and I know who they were to me, but… but I've forgotten their names. The longer I'm here, the less I remember about them, about our lives together."

I quit jogging. I realized I had no memory of other people, no family, no friends. Just a big house, a gun, and a pool of blood. I had been a successful businesswoman but what kind of person had I been?

Sam squatted and buried his face in his hands. "I can't. I can't go on. It's no use. Look around."

The canyon looked the same as when we returned to Wolf, but the woods had disappeared. Ahead, I saw outcroppings not far from where we stopped. I pulled Sam to his feet and led him there. It was time for a break.

Wolf continued along the rim when we stopped, but he returned and followed us into the rocks. Huge hunks of granite were scattered around with little paths between the stones. I pulled Sam among them. An area in the middle of the stones seemed protected from the stark reality that surrounded it. Soft grass grew in the most protected spot. I led Sam there, took off my leather cloak and spread it on the grass. The softness of the cloak magnified the softness of the grass underneath.

We sat side-by-side, our backs against one boulder. Wolf sandwiched himself between us. The warmth of his body was comforting. Sam buried his face against my shoulder, the tears flowing faster. I wrapped my arms around him and rocked him as one would a child. I petted his hair and murmured soothing, meaningless words. It was awkward, but I did not know what else to do.

After a long time, Sam's crying slowed, then stopped. He pulled away from me and wiped his nose and eyes on his sleeve. He didn't look at me, but stared straight ahead.

I wondered about the point of this journey. Our task seemed impossible. Anyway, what could the Queen of the Underworld do for us? She could not return us to our previous lives, and no part of this afterlife was appealing. What if we stayed here, among these boulders? We didn't need to eat. Perhaps if we sat long enough, we would turn into one of these stones.

Sam slumped against me. He appeared exhausted by his weeping. My own thoughts slowed as I wondered about this person I had been given as a compeer. He must have been a good man, kind to his family and others. Very different, I realized, from the hard businesswoman of my vision. I thought about the rest of my life and what led me to the fateful encounter of my death. As if emphasizing my bewilderment, I heard the mournful, mewing scream of an owl hunting.

CHAPTER 20

"Well, well, well, what do we have here?" I awoke to a deep growl and Wolf's whimper.

Before I even opened my eyes, I thought I recognized the slap of Volos's rod against his leather pants. When I looked up, I didn't see Volos but a swarthy man with curly black hair peeking out from under an ebony helmet.

I tried to sit up but my arms and legs were tangled with Sam's. We had fallen asleep. The guardian — or whoever he was — said nothing while Sam and I disentangled ourselves and stood.

"Greetings, sir." Sam smiled at him.

He was a fierce-looking man, not big, but powerfully built. His chest was bare, but he wore a length of soft leather wrapped into a skirt that hung to his knees. Fine leather gloves encased his hands and crawled up his arms. His helmet was a stylized head of a wolf. Its long pointed ears and snout made him appear demonic. In that moment I thought this guardian would be harder to tame than Wolf and his pack.

"What are you doing here?" the man growled. "Why are you not on the path? Weren't you told to stay on the path?"

"We-we got lost, sir," Sam stuttered.

"Sam was abducted, and Wolf and I went to save him, which we did. But we didn't know the way back to the path. We figured out how to get to the temple, but we ran into this canyon." I spilled the whole story out at once. "Can you help us?"

"Weren't you told to stay on the path?" the guardian snarled, as if he had not heard a word of my explanation.

I tried again, slower this time. "We were following our instructions," I said, my voice defiant, "but the deer-man grabbed Sam and carried him away into the forest."

"The deer-man?" The guardian frowned, anger clouding his dark features. He slapped a strange device against his thigh. It was about a foot long, shaped like the letter "T" with a loop on the top. The word "ankh" flashed through my mind.

"A person," I said, "wearing this deer skin with antlers on his head. He was being chased by the cat-men—people wearing panther pelts. Their leader said they were the tribe of the Stone Cold Panthers."

He nodded. "The lost ones," he murmured.

"The deer-man grabbed me and took me to this big meadow. Sara and Wolf and his pack followed." Sam dropped his hand toward the top of Wolf's head but Wolf had pressed himself into the dirt and continued to whimper. "I think they intended to save me, sir." Sam tried again to smile at the guardian, but the man seemed impervious to his charms. "The cat-man challenged me to a fight." "But Sam didn't have a weapon." I jumped back into the story.

"Sara saved me." Sam turned to smile at me.

"The cat-man wanted us to join him, but we refused." A pang of regret twisted my belly. Would it have been better to have joined the Panthers?

"He gave me this cloak." It was all we had to prove that we hadn't made up the whole thing.

"And now we're lost." Sam whispered this last.

A low growl rose out of the guardian's throat. "You know you're not supposed to leave the path, don't you?"

"Yes, sir," Sam said.

"But we couldn't help it," I said, softer now. What was he going to do to us? He looked angry and mean, slapping that ankh against his leg.

"Well, you can't stay here," he said after a long pause. "Gather up your things."

I slung my bag over my shoulder, then picked up the deer-skin cloak and wrapped it around myself. The guardian pointed his ankh through the standing stones, away from the canyon and away from Kore's Temple. Sam grabbed my hand as we were marched away from our destination. I could almost feel the box in Sam's bag trying to keep itself aimed at the temple as the temple itself disappeared behind us.

We walked and walked, Wolf sulking along beside Sam. He had quit whimpering. The guardian behind us kept slapping the ankh against his leg. I wondered if it burned like the rod Volos carried back at the workshop. I remembered the lightning that raced through my body when Volos used that rod on me. I wanted to protect both Sam and myself from that pain.

Ahead, the forest opened up. Then I saw it. A path. Was it *the* path? Sam squeezed my hand. He had seen it too.

"Stop here," the guardian said.

Like obedient children we did. How I wished later we hadn't been so obedient. How I wish I hadn't been so afraid of him. How I wish we had run away then. Run back to the path.

CHAPTER 21

"My name is Anubis." the guardian remained standing behind us. "These woods are my domain. My brother, The Baron, gave you something." He growled. "He sent me because you are no longer worthy couriers. He said to give it to me."

The name triggered a memory. An Egyptian tomb painting of the Jackal-Headed God leading a soul into the afterlife. He looked so benign in that image, but this guardian reminded me of an attacking wolf.

His voice was so commanding Sam was swinging his bag around to the front to open it. I put my hand on his arm, stopping him. Had I ever gotten away with defying a guardian? I imagined the pain this one was able to inflict on us, but we couldn't give him The Baron's box.

"No." I faced Anubis. "The Baron said we must deliver it to his sister, the Queen of the Dead. No one else."

"He changed his mind," the man snarled. "Give it to me." He slipped the ankh into a loop on his belt and held out both hands to Sam.

Sam looked at me. I shook my head. This felt wrong. More wrong than defying a guardian. I wondered why Anubis didn't grab Sam's bag, but then I remembered trying to pick up the box earlier. Sam had to give it to him. No one could take it.

"Look." Anubis pointed to our right. After all the walking and jogging we had done, we saw the wall of The Baron's palace. The door stood open. "Give it to me. You can escape from here and return to the Empyrean."

Through the doorway, I saw warm sunlight. There was green grass and the sound of a fountain. I even imagined I heard birds singing and tiny wind chimes calling my name, my real name, the name I didn't remember.

Sam looked from the Empyrean to me, back to the Empyrean, and then back to me. He wanted to go walk through that door. He wanted to escape from the gloom of the Nether Realm. Had he heard his real name, too?

I considered Anubis's proposition. But what was in the Empyrean for us? Sam may have been comforted by the pictures of his family he had found in the workshop, but for me, working at the loom had been torture. I wasn't eager to spend my eternity there trying to unravel my former life, my fingers bloodied. I didn't know what lay ahead, but Ankou had promised a next phase in this journey through the afterlife. In that moment I decided I would rather take my chances with Kore, the Queen of the Dead, than returning to the Empyrean at the prompting of this sinister guardian.

"No," I said, with more force this time. "The Baron gave it to us. We are the ones who must deliver it to his sister."

Anubis turned away from me to address Sam. He knew Sam carried the box and perceived his hesitation. I might be defiant, but it was Sam he had to convince.

"Are you letting her make your decisions for you?" Anubis said in that tone men use to persuade other men to ignore a woman's opinion. I recognized that tactic. Was it because I had been a businesswoman in my former life? "She doesn't have it." Anubis continued to ignore me. "You do. Give it to me." He held out his hands again.

Sam looked at me, his eyes pleading. I shook my head. Ankou had said we could never return to the Empyrean. Anubis was lying to Sam, to both of us. I let my palm slide down Sam's arm and squeezed his hand. Whatever happened, we were in this together.

The forest fell silent, holding its breath. I saw a grayish-brown owl glide behind Anubis and land on the upper branch of a tree. It twisted its head this way and that. Sam squeezed my hand as though he had made a decision.

"No." Sam pulled himself straighter. "Sara's right, we are the ones who must deliver it." Ever the peacemaker, he continued, "but you're welcome to travel with us."

Anubis burst out laughing. "I am welcome to travel with you. You defy me in my own kingdom. Then ask me to tag along on this futile quest?" His laughter turned into an ominous growl, but he couldn't take the box. I thought that would keep us safe.

"No," he barked. "Sit down. Give me your daggers."

He pushed, and in spite of our earlier defiance we sat. Like obedient children, we unstrapped our weapons and handed them to him. He hung them in a nearby tree. Then he took the ankh from his belt and jammed it into the ground until all that showed was the circle at the top. While we watched, mesmerized, he slipped a braided leather thong through the loop, then tied the ends around our ankles, my left, Sam's right, with six inches apart. After my initial compliance, I kicked and pulled but that only tightened the cord. We were pinned.

"You two are not going anywhere," Anubis snarled, standing up and looking at us. "Call for me when you change your minds. Maybe I'll came back and release you. Otherwise, you will face The Baron's wrath when he learns that you have defied me and failed him."

With that, he walked away. The wall with the open door and vision of the Empyrean disappeared as he passed it. After a moment, he vanished around a bend in the path.

I looked at Sam. What had I done? I reached out and touched the top of the ankh. A bolt of lightning shot up my arm and through the rest of my body. I gasped. Then I grabbed the thong, one hand on each side of the rod to use it to wrench the ankh free. After watching my futile efforts for a moment, Sam added his strength to mine. Not even a hint of movement. We were tied together and pinned to this spot.

My earlier bravado evaporated. "I-I'm so sorr–" "No," Sam stopped me. "you were right. It was a trick and I would have fallen for it." He leaned over and put his arm around me. "However bad this looks, that would have been worse."

We both gazed down the path where the wall had been. Sam was right, but I wished it wasn't so. In that moment I wished we had been able to return to the Empyrean of green grass, singing birds, and wind chimes that knew our real names.

CHAPTER 22

We had defied Anubis and now we were immobilized on the edge of the path, at least I assumed it was *the* path. We couldn't go forward to the Temple of the Queen of the Dead and we couldn't return to the Empyrean. It looked like we would spend eternity in this limbo, forever caught in the Nether Realm. Would other people traveling this path see us and be warned? Could they help us? Did other people travel this path between Empyrean and Kore's Temple? There must be traffic of some sort along this path, someone besides Anubis, the deer-man and his followers, and us. It looked well travelled, even though we had seen no one else.

I realized I had expected the path to be part of Anubis's lie. I thought it would disappear when he did. But it remained. Enticingly close, yet impossibly far away.

Sam still had his arm around me. His silent touch gave warm comfort in this hard, cold place. I opened my cloak, scooted over, and wrapped it around us. Wolf lay down next to Sam, content to stay with us though he could leave. I slid my arm around Sam's waist, and we held each other, lost in our own thoughts. I continued to stare at the path as though something, someone, would appear to help us. But no one did. The forest surrounding us appeared abandoned and colorless. The trees, and bushes, and underbrush were all shades of gray, as was the path. Everything appeared dead. There was no bird song, no movement of tiny creatures in the underbrush. No deer-man or the cat-men that chased him, no pack of friendly wolves. We were alone, with only each other for company. Was the owl still watching us? I was afraid to look. Had everyone abandoned us?

Silent tears leaked from my eyes. I wept for all that might have been, for the life that led me to this place of loneliness and abandonment. I remembered little of my previous life, but I wept for the futility of it. That big office, my beautiful house, the power, all had evaporated in one gun shot. It did not matter if my murderer was a burglar, a home invader come to attack me in my home, a former lover, or disgruntled employee. Even though I had a gun, I had died. I didn't know what happened, but there was no way to go back and make things right.

I remembered no family or friends, no lovers, no one I cared about and no one who cared about me. Had I died alone and unmourned? Had I brought my life's emptiness into the afterlife with me? I mourned for the self I left behind, even if I only remembered brief snippets. I mourned for what might have been. When my tears slowed, I wiped my nose on the sleeve of my tunic.

Sam was a victim, too. Shot by the police, he said. Was he a thief? A gangster or a criminal? He didn't seem the type of person who would have a run-in with the cops. He said his family wanted to clear his name. Had he been shot by mistake, too? Maybe neither one of us was supposed to be here. Could the Queen of the Dead make things right for us? Could she turn back time and return us to our lives? What had The Baron meant when he said she could guide us to the next phase of our journey?

Sam pulled me closer, and I buried my tear-stained face in his tunic. I was tired of what Anubis called our futile quest, tired of all I had been asked to do and endure since I woke up on that boat. Weren't the dead supposed to rest? Perhaps the Queen of the Dead would just let us be.

But we would never meet the Queen unless someone came to free us, and that didn't appear likely. We were stranded. Was the Nether Realm full of people like us? People who shouldn't be here but couldn't find a way out? Were there more people like the Stone Cold Panthers who gave up and instead chased each other through these woods?

Using his free hand Sam wiped away the tears drying on my cheeks.

"We still have each other." He seemed to read my despair. "You aren't alone here. Whatever happens, we're in this together." He motioned to the hobble holding us to the ground and laughed. "I couldn't leave if I wanted."

That should have made me feel better, but I was trapped in an afterlife I didn't understand and couldn't escape. I may have been a successful businesswoman before my death, but here, I was powerless, unable to control my fate. Doomed to this dark and dreary nightmare.

An urgent wail erupted from deep in my chest followed by a new deluge of tears. I buried my face in Sam's shoulder and cried until the front of his tunic was soaking wet and I had no more tears.

He must have been a good father. He rocked me, murmuring soft, meaningless words into my ear. "There, there, *compañera. Estas bien.* Don't cry, *querida. Estoy aqui.* Shh, shh."

When I stopped crying, he used the edge of his tunic to dry my face. Then he finger-combed as much of my hair as he could reach.

"We still have the box and each other," he whispered. "Together we've conquered every other obstacle. We'll find a way around this."

He cupped my face in his hand and kissed my forehead, then pulled me down onto the cloak and wrapped his arms around me. "Rest now," he murmured. "When you feel better, we'll figure out how to continue our journey."

His whole being radiated a protective love that warmed me in spite of the desolate world around me. I closed my eyes and fell into a deep sleep.

CHAPTER 23

I'm standing at the head of a conference table. I am prepared for this meeting. As usual, I'm perfectly dressed. My fuchsia business suit is impeccably tailored, the coral blouse underneath open just enough to show a hint of the cleavage I am so proud of. My hair, makeup, nails are perfect. I am ready for the reporters who will find and question me later. Their photographs will show me in the most advantageous light.

The room is dark except for the chart projected on the wall behind me. The news isn't good. Our investors had never expected that we would be profitable this soon — few startups like ours were — but now they insist we improve our bottom line by lowering our costs. Everyone — at least those seated around the table in front of me — knows that changes have to be made. Today is the beginning of the next phase in the life of this company. My company.

I have called my management team together to share how deep we will cut. No one in this room is at risk. Our salaries are safe. But after today things will be different.

A fifteen percent reduction did not sound like much when I met with the investors earlier.

"Every company's got fat," one of them had said. "We're just asking you to trim a little, darling." His tone was calculated to put me in my place, but I refused to take the bait. There would be time for revenge later.

Of course, what our investors considered frivolous and expendable, the people around this table see as important to the morale of our employees. But I had agreed to make these cuts to improve our financials in preparation for our IPO. A good stock price will benefit the investors and everyone in this room. And we know it.

I distribute the lists and the final descriptions of the severance packages I negotiated with my HR people. The packages wouldn't cost that much. I worked with each department head, identifying who would stay and who would have to go. Many of our staff are contractors. They are already in their own meetings. We will retain some, but many will pack up the few personal items they are allowed to bring on site. They won't be getting a severance package.

This is a cost-cutting measure, so the employee benefits are being cut as well. It is the nature of the business. Everyone took a chance working for a start-up. In the end, some benefit more than others.

"You know what you have to do." My voice is cold and hard. Some people call me "the ice queen" behind my back, but I've always known how to do what has to be done. I don't care what they think. Besides, soon that IPO will prove me right.

"We'll regroup tomorrow," I continue, "and strategize our next steps." With that I turn to walk out of the room.

When I touch the door handle, lightning-sharp pain flows up my leg.

I jerked awake. The peach pit was bouncing on my chest. Its tiny pin pricks magnified the stinging in my foot. I looked down. Sam had turned in his sleep, pulling our hobble until my ankle touched Anubis's ankh. I pulled my leg away from it.

I had been dreaming. No longer was I the elegant businesswoman. Instead I was in the Nether Realm, pinned at the edge of the forest, mere steps from the path that was supposed to lead us to the gleaming temple. Lost and alone, unable to complete the assignment The Baron had given us, unable to move on to the next phase of our afterlives. I could feel the dried tears from my earlier breakdown.

"Hey." Sam touched my arm. "Bad dream?"

I shook my head. My dream had been good. It was my present that was bad.

"I've been thinking." He pulled us up into a seated position. "Your guardian — what was his name?"

"Ankou?" I asked.

"Yes, Ankou. Remember, he said we had what we needed."

Ankou could not have known what Anubis would do to us.

"And maybe we do," Sam persisted. "Maybe we do have what we need."

Shaking my head, I scooted away from Sam, reached over and pulled my bag closer. He did the same, leaving an expanse of the leather cloak between us.

I took my things out of the bag. There wasn't much — my notebook, a pencil, and the coin we had used earlier. Flipping through my notebook, I discovered a new image, a woman in a fuchsia suit. My dream had something to do with my previous life, but I didn't have time right now to consider how that fit into what I knew. That would not help free us. I snapped the notebook shut.

Sam reached into his bag and set The Baron's box next to his pinned leg. He dumped his notebook and a pencil onto the cloak.

Nothing new or useful tumbled out of either bag. We studied our paltry possessions. I looked at the daggers hanging out of reach. If we had them, it would be so simple to cut the thongs that held us and escape.

Sam picked up The Baron's box and waved it over the pile. "Become something useful." When nothing changed, he touched the tip of the box to Anubis's ankh. "Ouch!" He jerked the box back. "Not smart." He laughed, setting it on my cloak. Picking up his notebook, he waved it over the ankh. "Abracadabra." He touched the edge to the ankh then jerked the notebook back. He laughed again and dropped it into his bag.

"Wolf," I pointed toward the ankh, "make yourself helpful."

Wolf wagged his tail.

"You're useless." Sam ruffed the top of Wolf's head.

I considered the small pile of our things. How was Anubis able to hold that thing when it burned us?

I looked toward the ankh and back to the pile again. I released the leather arm guard from my left hand. Holding it between my thumb and forefinger I touched it to the ankh. Then pulled it back. "Nothing," I touched it to the ankh again.

"Leather," Sam said. "That's why Anubis wears those leather gloves and skirt."

I nodded. "That's why the hobble is leather. Of course."

Sam took the arm guard and tried to jam it into the circle of the ankh but it didn't fit. He tried to wrap it around the hoop but it was too stiff. He handed it back.

If we had leather gloves, we might grab the wretched thing and pull it out of the ground. But we didn't. We continued to stare at the ankh.

Suddenly, Sam shouted, "Ankou was right."

He scooted off the cloak. The cloak the deer-man had given me. My soft, warm, leather cloak.

Sam folded its edge several layers thick and dropped it over the ankh. Using both hands, he grabbed it and pulled, wiggling the ankh back and forth.

At first nothing. Then it moved, an inch, two inches. He kept working until it popped out. We were free. Sam leaned over and hugged me. My compeer had liberated us.

Our legs were still hobbled together with the ankh hanging between them. We stood up and stutter-stepped to our daggers, dragging the ankh behind us. It didn't take much to cut through the thongs that formed the hobble.

Sam stopped me from tossing the mutilated pieces deep into the forest. "We should keep these." He took them out of my hand.

I nodded. He was right. We each dropped one piece into our bags.

We strapped on our daggers and pulled our bags over our shoulders. Before I could pick up the cloak, Sam stopped me again.

He said pointing toward the ankh lying on the ground. "What should we do with this?"

I never wanted to touch that thing again, but it made sense to take it. Wrapping it in the cloak, I stuffed the ankh into my bag.

After looking around to be sure we didn't leave anything, I walked to the path.

"Which way?" I asked. I couldn't see the Temple.

Sam pulled out The Baron's box and balanced it on his palm. It remained motionless for a moment and then pointed up the trail, away from the direction Anubis had taken.

Nodding, I grabbed Sam's free hand and stepped on the path. I didn't know where we were going, but continuing our journey felt right.

CHAPTER 24

We walked, then jogged until the path took an upward turn. Without a word, we stopped, caught our breath, then continued at a slower pace. We strolled together in silence, lost in our own thoughts.

The twisting trail took us deep into the forest and up another ridge. Wolf disappeared into the woods several times and then returned farther up the path.

I thought about my past and everything that had happened since waking up on Charon's boat. The motto above the door at The Baron's Palace demanded, "Remember, Release, Return." I did remember at least some portions of my life and death. I could let them go. I was making a new life here, wherever "here" was. But what did it mean, "return"? We couldn't return. There was no way back to Empyrean. Anubis had only offered us an illusion. Even if we turned around, there was no way through the door to the Baron's Palace. No way across the river.

We had to continue forward, to the Queen of the Dead. Her temple was the most beautiful thing I'd seen here, but I knew things were not always as they appeared. I had thought Empyrean would be delightful, too.

"All those years in church." I interrupted the silence. I remembered being a child, sitting in hot, crowded pews, while an overwrought pastor ranted. "After all those sermons, all those threats of hellfire and damnation, all those flowery descriptions of heaven…" I waved my hand at the dark, dismal forest. "This is not what I expected."

Sam looked around and nodded.

"Actually," I continued, "in spite of everything we've been through, this has been much more interesting than any description of, of — where we are, anyway? The Empyrean wasn't heaven, and this, well, as awful as this is, it doesn't seem like hell either. Did all those preachers for all those years have it wrong? I've never heard of the Bardo. Are we really dead or is this a shared hallucination?"

Sam shook his head. "I don't know, *compañera*." He slipped his hand into mine. We continued to walk together in silence.

"Tell me what you remember of your life… before. I was a successful businesswoman. But I wasn't very nice. My employees called me 'the Ice queen'."

Sam stopped and pulled his hand away from mine. "You were the Ice Queen?" His eyes widened. "You were the one who got me killed?" Then he shook his head. "No, *compañera*, that couldn't have been you."

I didn't see how I could have killed Sam. I was the one who had been murdered. But then, I didn't remember everything. Had I said too much and ruined the relationship with my only companion here in the afterlife? My stomach twisted. I longed to pull back my last words but there was nothing to do but continue.

We walked together to some nearby rocks and sat cross-legged, facing each other without touching. Wolf lay pressed against my thigh, comforting me. I told Sam about my dreams and visions. When I described the young man I hired with my low-ball offer, he looked away from me and back toward the path.

"I think I was that person. I thought working for you would be a great opportunity." He smiled as though the memory was a good one. "Then you let us go." The smile disappeared as he continued. "I was devastated. My family was devastated."

"But…" I wanted to justify my actions.

Sam touched my knees. "I lost everything when you fired me. And you lost everything when the bubble burst."

I had not remembered that, but it felt right when he said it. Instead of saving my company, I had destroyed it. And I destroyed others, including this gentle man who so loved his family.

I fingered the peach pit hanging above my cleavage. It was still prickly to touch, but did not hurt as much as I remembered. I let it drop back against my chest. The pain sharpened my feeling of guilt. Was it my fault we were here wandering through the Nether Realm? Did a more extreme punishment await me at the end of our quest? Even if I did not remember what happened?

"I didn't lose everything." I refused to admit what I knew must be true. "I lived in a big house."

"It wasn't yours anymore." His voice sounded so flat. Whatever emotions he felt about dying had drained away.

I remembered moving boxes piled around me. "And you came to my house to… to…" I could not continue. Had he been angry that I fired him? Why else would he accost me in the middle of the night? Yet, the murderer of my vision did not fit with the Sam I knew.

He closed his eyes as if imagining the scene. "I'd taken my family to a birthday party for my father-in-law. We had car trouble going home. I was looking for a phone. I didn't know it was your house, but the light was on."

"I always slept with a light on," I remembered. "I was afraid of sleeping alone in the dark." Closing my eyes I remembered that night. "Someone was pounding on my front door. I called the police, but I had my own protection."

Sam nodded. "You met me with a gun. I should have left then, but I recognized you. I don't think you knew who I was. You thought I was a stranger."

"I did know who you were, but I thought you had come to rob or even kill me. I had treated you so badly."

"As I remember it, we struggled for the gun. Somehow you were killed."

I touched the point on my chest where the bullet must have entered. The sharp pain I'd felt earlier was now only a dull ache.

"The police saw me holding your gun and shot me."

I opened my eyes and looked into Sam's face. He looked back at me. I expected him to be enraged, but all I saw was sadness. We both had died, and now we were compeers in the Nether Realm. How we got here didn't matter. Even Wolf sleeping next to me appeared untouched by our revelations.

In fact, I was surprised at how dispassionate we both were. We had caused each other's deaths. We should have been angry at each other, ourselves, the fates that had brought us together that night. But here we were discussing those events as though it were a story on TV.

"We were both supposed to die that night." I remembered what Aurora said when I first arrived at the pier. She had thought there would be another person with me.

He nodded. "I should have died on your porch, but I didn't. My family kept me on life support for a couple days. It was hopeless, of course. Finally, they agreed to pull the plug. They probably still think I am a murderer." Tears leaked from his eyes.

Our deaths had been the culmination of a series of horrible, tragic mistakes. A deep-rooted sadness roiled in my stomach. I may have been mistaken about Sam that night, but now I thought of the promise I'd seen in the young man in my visions. I remembered feeling that someday I wanted to work more closely with him. And now, here we were, compeers, making our way through the afterworld together.

Grabbing Sam's hands, I pulled him toward me. "I'm sorry," I said through my own tears. "I'm so, so sorry."

CHAPTER 25

Wolf woke as Sam and I cried in each other's arms. He looked from one of us to the other, whining and licking our faces as though he could curb our tears.

I cried for what was and what might have been. I cried for who I had been, what I had done, and all the people like Sam I had hurt. Sam probably cried for his lost family and perhaps other parts of his life. I cried for the family I could not remember. We both cried for lives cut short.

I wanted to make our deaths Sam's fault. Why had he come to my house that night? Why hadn't he left when I told him to? Why had he struggled with me for the gun? But I was at fault too. Why did I even have a gun? Why hadn't I waited for the police? Why had I thought the worst about one of my most promising employees? So many questions. Questions with no answers.

I wanted to be angry about how my life ended, about my unfinished business, about who I could have become. I wondered if Sam wanted to be angry, too. He had such promise. Now that promise was lost.

But none of that seemed important any more. We could not undo what had been done. I thought about my impression when I first met Sam, that he would be a fine associate. I had few real friends in life. But perhaps now I could change that.

In spite of the circumstances of our deaths, Sam and I had been good companions on this journey through the Nether Realm. Would that end, now that he knew who I had been? Could I do in the afterlife what I had not been able to do earlier? Could I become a true partner to my companion?

I was not sure how to proceed, but I didn't want to continue alone. I resolved to do whatever it took to convince Sam that we should go on together.

When our tears stopped, Sam disentangled his body from mine and pushed away from me. His eyes were dry although his face was still tear-streaked. He gazed past me toward the path.

Here it comes, I thought. I rallied my arguments for remaining compeers.

Sam watched a grayish-brown owl glide overhead and land on a tree in front of us. "We can't go back, can we? We can't change who we were or what we did. We can't even make amends for… for…"

I wondered if this was the end of everything. Would he take The Baron's box and continue on his own, leaving me behind? What did I expect? We were responsible for each other's deaths. Why wouldn't we split up and find our separate ways to Kore's Temple?

I thought Sam would resume crying, but there was a new strength in his eyes as though he'd come to some resolution. He would take The Baron's box and continue on alone.

He was right. There was no escape from this place. Anubis's vision of the Empyrean had been an illusion.

But it had taken both of us to get to this place. "We have to finish this." I watched his reaction. "We need to see what the Queen of the Dead says." I clung to The Baron's demand that we had to work together and Aurora's promise that there was more to the afterlife than what we had experienced so far.

Sam rummaged in his bag and pulled out the leather thong that had bound our legs. "I know now it wasn't an accident that The Baron has made us companions. Give me your arm."

When I held out my left arm, he slipped the thong around my wrist and tightened it. We gazed into each other's eyes.

"We are more than companions, more than friends, more than family," he said. "I am your compeer… forever."

I looked at the thong, then back to Sam. He wasn't going on without me. He wanted to remain compeers. Then I thought about the motto above the door of the Baron's palace, "Remember, Release, Return." We remembered what brought us to this place. Now it was time to release our past lives. I could not change what happened but I could become a better companion.

I pulled my half of the leather hobble out of my bag, and nodded to Sam. He held out his right arm, and I tied the thong around his wrist.

"We are more than companions, more than friends, more than family." I looked into Sam's eyes, dry and steady now, and whispered, "I am your compeer… forever."

He intertwined his thumb with mine and wrapped his fingers around my palm until our two hands made a single fist. After a moment, we did a quick downward movement and broke apart. "Forever," we said in unison, laughing. Wolf gave a yelp as though agreeing with us.

When we stood up to return to the path, the string holding the peach pit around my neck broke. I caught it. It lay lifeless in my palm. Its rough surface no longer stung my fingertips.

I held out my hand to show Sam. "It died."

He held a similar pit. "Mine, too."

I considered re-tying it around my neck but then realized it must have served its purpose, and I dropped it into my bag. Following my lead, he did the same.

Sam pulled out The Baron's box to verify the direction, but we both could see that the path led upward even though the trees blocked our view. I took Sam's hand, and we moved forward, together. Wolf trotted in front of us, leading the way.

I was still sorting out the revelations about our past lives, my relationship with Sam, and the commitment we had made to each other. Since we had solved the mystery of our deaths, perhaps we had achieved some cosmic goal of our afterlives and the rest of our journey would be uneventful.

I was wrong again.

CHAPTER 26

As we walked, I considered my companions, my compeer Sam, and Wolf who had been with us since our first steps away from The Baron's Palace. I understood now why Sam and I were thrown together. Although we barely knew each other before we died, this journey in the afterlife had brought us close. What would Kore, the Queen of the Dead, make of us? Would she let us stay together, as we had pledged, or did we have separate futures? We both meant what we had said, but would we be able to honor our promises to each other?

The woods were changing. There was a slight chill in the air and tendrils of mist appeared between the trees like diminutive ghosts watching our progress. Soon a cloud came out of the forest and onto the path, swirling around our ankles.

The fog in front of us obscured everything, Sam and I stopped. Wolf disappeared into the fog ahead as though nothing had changed. Expecting him to return, we waited, but he didn't come back. It was as if he had never existed.

Sam released my hand and pulled The Baron's box out of his bag. Perhaps we had missed a turn and were going the wrong direction. No matter which way he pointed the box, it turned on his palm until it was pointing straight ahead.

He put it back into his bag, took my left hand and stepped forward. I dropped my right hand to my dagger, taking it from of its sheath and holding it at my side, prepared for whatever awaited.

The fog was a silvery blanket, moving aside as we inched forward. No sounds escaped the forest. The path unfurled in front of us and disappeared behind us. My uneasiness calmed as we moved forward without incident.

Then I heard something. A dog whimpering. Sam squeezed my hand.

The fog opened to a strange tableau. Anubis, wearing his leather skirt and the helmet with the pointed ears and snout, stood in the middle of the path. A pack of wolves, including Wolf, surrounded him. Wolf was trying to come to us but Anubis had his left hand buried in his ruff, holding him at his side.

"You got yourselves free I see." Anubis's voice was a low growl.

I knew why Wolf whimpered. I wanted to cringe and look away, too. When Sam squeezed my hand, I regained some courage.

"Yes, sir." I forced myself to meet the guardian's eyes.

"And what did you do with my ankh? Did you toss it into the forest?"

"No, sir." I wondered if it would have been better to have thrown the strange device away. I felt its weight at the bottom of my bag.

I continued to glare at him, unwilling to bow to his obvious superior position. His mouth twitched as though he were trying to conceal a smile. However, before we could see where this contest of wills would lead, a low growl vibrated the wolf pack. A person with an antler headdress appeared out of the fog behind us. What looked like members of the Stone Cold Panthers followed him. Each man carried a long pointed spear. The deer-man skidded to a stop next to Sam and me while the rest of his gang surrounded us.

The deer-man stepped forward, set down his spear and squatted, placing his palms on the path and bowing his head toward Anubis. From his grimy white tunic and trousers, I knew he was a person like us. I wondered if he was the same deer-man we'd met earlier, but he didn't look familiar.

"Sire," he whispered.

Anubis slapped his free hand against his leather skirt. It was obvious he missed the ankh hidden in the deerskin in my bag. When he touched the deer-man's head, the man raised himself into a seated squat. While I glared at Anubis, the deer-man kept his gaze lowered, as if he feared the guardian.

"What are you doing here?" Anubis snarled.

Without answering, deer-man turned away from Anubis, stood up, and looked at Sam and me.

"Where is it?" he asked Sam, ignoring me.

Sam shook his head. I wondered what the deer-man was looking for.

"Where is it? Where is the Pallium of Power?" the man demanded.

Again Sam shook his head. He dropped my hand and held his hands open in front of him.

"We-we don't have it," I said, drawing his attention from my compeer. "We don't even know what you are talking about."

The deer-man stepped forward and slapped me. "Don't lie." He raised his nose and sniffws the air. "I can smell it on you."

I still held my dagger. With one swift move I might wound or even kill this man if he could be killed.

Sam's hand touched my left arm, advising caution. He was right. Perhaps what we needed was his subtlety, not my aggression. These Panthers, Anubis, and the wolf pack surrounded us. Beyond Sam, and maybe Wolf, I had no idea who my allies might be.

Sam slid his hand down my arm, enfolded it around mine and pulled the two of us closer to the deer-man.

"We don't know what you're talking about." Sam's voice had the same slow even sound he had used when we first met Wolf. "If you tell us what you're looking for, we could help you find it." An unlikely promise, but I realized it wasn't the words that mattered at that moment, but the tone.

"Open your bags," the deer-man said at last, his command ruined as his voice broke. He sounded like a boy playing a man.

I glanced at Anubis, but he seemed to enjoy the confrontation. He nodded for us to continue.

Sam and I stepped back and swung our bags off our shoulders in a single motion. Sam squatted, pulling me down with him. He opened his bag, put out his notebook, the dried-up peach pit, and The Baron's box. Was that what this man was looking for?

The man ignored the box and turned to me. Sheathing my dagger, I pulled out my notebook, then felt around until I found the coin and the peach pit, and set them on my notebook. I pulled out the ankh still wrapped in the leather cloak.

"Aha." The man grabbed the cloak and spilled the ankh onto the ground. Ignoring Anubis's, he flung the cloak over his head and then dropped it on my shoulders.

"The Pallium," he shouted to the mass of cat-men. His tone changed to one of reverence.

The cat-men fell to their knees, pressing their foreheads to the ground. "The Pallium," they cried.

The deer-man turned to Anubis. "Sire, she has to come with us. She took the Pallium. Now she must be our leader."

Anubis's face told me something wasn't right, but he nodded again.

A skullcap with a long thong tied under his chin held the antlers on the deer-man's head. He reached up, undid the string, took the antlers off and held them as an offering.

Unsure of what was going on, I reached to take them from him.

"You were a worthy opponent. You accepted the Pallium. You have to be our leader." He looked up at Anubis, then back at me, his eyes begging. "Now you must set me free."

Here was someone who recognized me, the true me, the me who had been an important person before my death. I could be the first deer-woman here in the Nether Realm. The thought warmed me. I had been the first woman to achieve important honors before. What would it mean to be the queen of the cat-men?

"Don't," Sam cried, slapping my arm away.

"No," the deer-man screamed as he juggled the antlers before regaining his hold on them.

"Don't take that," Sam said, loud enough for the man to hear. "It's a trap. If you accept these antlers, you'll become the deer-man and be caught here, maybe forever."

I considered what he said. That didn't seem so bad. The queen of the cat-men. It had a certain ring.

Then I remembered my pledge to Sam. Would he continue without me? If I took this man's place would he become Sam's new companion? Would he accompany Sam to Kore's Temple instead of me? Would I be trapped in the Nether Realm forever?

"Give him back his Pallium," Sam said, his voice low, calm.

I touched the soft leather of the cloak, remembering the times it had embraced me, embraced us. Except for Sam's friendship, it was the only pleasure I had found in my afterlife. I was reluctant to release its softness. But after a moment I slipped it off and set it in front of the deer-man. Caressing it one last time, I stepped back to stand with Sam.

We stood looking at the miserable young man.

"Leave the cloak and your antlers," Sam said to him. "Come with us to Kore's Temple." He looked at the cat-men surrounding us. "All of you, come with us."

I was surprised. Wasn't our mission our own? We had learned so much about each other and become true partners. What would happen if these people joined us?

"No," the deer-man said. He looked at Anubis, then back at me. "I can't leave unless you take my place." He sounded both desperate and pathetic. I didn't know what held him here, but I realized his offer had been a ruse. And I didn't want to be caught in that trap.

I shook my head, taking Sam's hand.

Wailing, the man made one last appeal to Anubis who also shook his head. The deer-man retied the antlers onto his head. He picked up the cloak and his spear. He led his gang back into the fog, leaving us alone with Anubis and his pack of wolves.

CHAPTER 27

In one smooth motion, keeping his hold on Wolf, Anubis picked up the ankh.

When he stood up, his smirk faded, replaced by an unreadable facade. The soft rumble of the wolves behind him pointed out the danger of our position. This guardian had tempted us to leave our quest once and then pinned us to the side of the path when we refused his offer. What would he do to us now?

Anubis released Wolf and faced the rest of the pack. With a low growl he spread his arms, appearing to dismiss them. They turned and slid into the fog. Soon only Wolf remained, looking from Anubis to us. I squeezed Sam's hand before he could call Wolf. More going on here than I understood.

"This one has been a good companion for you two." Anubis turned back toward us and rested his palm on Wolf's head. "But now it is time for him to return to his pack." A low snarl crept out of the guardian's throat.

Wolf crouched, as though trying to make himself as flat as possible, and whimpered. From deep in the fog, another wolf howled.

"Go." Anubis pushed Wolf with his foot. Wolf yelped, then stood, and glided up the path. Soon he, too, disappeared into the mist. Sorrow filled me. Just as I had grown to love Sam, I had developed a fondness toward Wolf. Now he was gone.

Sam and I were alone with the guardian who tapped his ankh against his thigh. I held my breath. Would he punish us now?

"You two have been very resourceful," he said at last. "You have remembered your lives and your deaths."

We nodded. I didn't remember everything about my life, but my death and Sam's part in it were clear in my mind.

"You've released the emotions surrounding your past." It was more of a statement than a question.

Sam and I looked at each other. We understood both of us carried some fault for our deaths. Not only had we forgiven each other, we had become true compeers.

"Pick up your things," Anubis said.

I scooped up my notebook, the peach pit, and the coin, dropped them into my bag and then slipped the strap over my head.

Sam put his notebook and peach pit into his bag.

"Not The Baron's Box," Anubis barked.

Holding the box in one fist, Sam grabbed my hand with the other.

"You refused me earlier." Anubis's face darkened. "You remember how that turned out. Will you refuse me again?"

I squeezed Sam's hand. This was it, the end of our journey.

I nodded, afraid to speak.

"What?" Anubis growled.

"No-no, sir," I whispered. Then I pulled myself up straight. I remembered the person I had been. If now was to be when we truly died, I wanted to do it as that strong woman. "The Baron said we must give the box to his sister, the Queen of the Dead. No one else." Again, I looked the guardian full in the face, daring him to challenge our mission.

A growl rumbled from his throat. Sam squeezed my hand, but it was too late. After everything we had been through, I would not back down now.

"Did The Baron tell you why he didn't take the box to Kore's Temple himself?" Anubis cocked his head in such a way it appeared he knew the answer and he knew we didn't.

I shook my head. We were pawns taken by our guardians to The Baron's palace, and then sent by him into the Nether Realm on this journey to Kore's Temple. We had not been in a position to ask questions, not to someone as powerful and important as The Baron.

Without breaking eye contact, I pondered. Why would The Baron depend on us, people who were dead and appeared lost in the Bardo? Why would he entrust Sam and me with such a valuable object? He must have known the dangers we would face. I felt stupid. It was not in my nature to be so compliant, so trusting. And yet I had complied. We both had.

But Anubis was not finished asking his questions. "Did The Baron tell you that what was hidden inside his box would make you special, even a guardian like us?"

I shook my head again as I remembered the last time Anubis wanted us to give him The Baron's box. Did he know what it contained? He acted like it was something remarkable. Did he know? Or was this another test?

"No," Sam said. "The Baron instructed us to take his box to Kore's Temple and give it to her. He didn't tell us what was in the box. He told us not to open it. And we haven't." His voice was stronger than I expected.

Anubis shook his head, smiled and then broke out into booming laughter that echoed off the surrounding mountains. "Where does The Baron find such simple and trusting souls?" he muttered, as if to himself.

I bristled at his description of us. Then I realized he was right. Even though I fought Aurora and Sigrún at every turn back in the Empyrean, I had not questioned the things they told me. I had gone along with Ankou and The Baron, not questioning them either.

Sam was less of a fighter than I was. I doubted he had challenged his guardians or even raised a single objection. Neither of us protested at The Baron's palace or later when we were pushed out into the Nether Realm. Perhaps Anubis was right, maybe we were just simple, trusting, and, I would add, stupid.

Anubis brought his mirth under control. "Aren't you curious?" He looked from Sam to me and back again.

I glanced at Sam. I was not sure where Anubis was going with his questions, but I thought we might as well follow him to the end, so I nodded.

Sam dropped my hand so he could hold the box in front of us.

"Well, what do you think?" Anubis winked. "Shouldn't we open it before you continue on your journey?"

I looked at the box, balanced on Sam's palm. Exquisite carvings were visible on all the sides. In addition to the skeleton on the top was laid out as if in a coffin, deer man and his cat-men followers on one side and a pack of wolves on the other, at the narrow top of the box was the image of a Grecian temple with a wavy line that looked like water. Sam turned the box so I could see the picture on the foot of the box. It was a tiny pool, surrounded by soft sand and living trees. It was not like anything we had seen either in Empyrean or in the Nether Realm. I had not realized until that moment I had seen no flowing water since stepping off that boat and onto the pier. It was strange that all the images related to our experiences in the Nether Realm, except that one. I wanted to ask Anubis what it meant, but before I could work out a question, he spoke.

"Look at the bottom."

Sam turned the box over. Like the top, it showed a stylized human figure. However, this person appeared to be alive. He (or she, it was hard to tell) wore a long gown cut full enough to hide the body. The skull had been replaced with a human face complete with tiny features, including eyes, nose, mouth, even eyebrows. Simple carved pupils replaced the demonic red stone eyes on the top of the box. The hands and feet had also been enfleshed, and the posture had changed. Where the person on the top of the box appeared to be lying down, perhaps in his own coffin, this one seemed to be standing. His (or her) feet were flat and the arms spread in a welcoming or triumphant gesture.

"That's the secret of the box. The promise of resurrection, rebirth." He growled. "But The Baron, King of the Dead, ruler of Empyrean, did not tell you that, did he? He tried to hide the true nature of the box and its contents from you, did he not?"

Sam and I looked at the box and its carvings, including the jubilant figure on its bottom. I looked at Sam now holding the box in both hands, twisting and turning it to look at the images. Was he thinking what I was thinking? Had we been duped? Could we have avoided everything we had suffered by opening the box and taking the contents for ourselves? Sam rubbed his thumb back and forth on the clasp as though considering whether to open it. Before he could decide, Anubis interrupted our thoughts.

"The Baron knows whoever owns this box and its contents has the gift of life in this place of death. You could be like him, like all of the guardians in the Bardo." Silence encircled us, as if the forest and its creatures were holding their collective breaths.

"We guardians were once souls like you," Anubis continued, his voice a soft caress. "Now we are gods, as you could be."

Sam and I were close to our goal. We had seen the Temple before walking into this fog. However, The Baron had made no promise of a reward for completing our quest. He had told us not to open the box but to give it to his sister, Kore, the Queen of the Dead. He had not threatened us but implied a penalty if we failed to deliver it. Had he been lying? Had we suffered needlessly? Could the box have made us guardians like Aurora and Sigrún and Anubis? Were we fools not to have opened it and taken for ourselves whatever was inside?

"We can't," Sam said at long last. "We've traveled so far."

Anubis growled again. "Then give me the box." He held out his hands. "I will protect you from what is to come."

My stomach clenched as I thought of my time in the Empyrean and my journey with Sam. Now Anubis suggested that our quest was not near completion. I was exhausted. Our stint in the forest of the Nether Realm and everything we had endured here weighed on me.

"You deserve to rest," Anubis echoed my thoughts, "after what you've been through."

For a moment, he looked like a kind uncle offering us a release from all we had suffered. I reached to take The Baron's box from Sam, intending to open it at long last.

"No." Sam enclosed it in his palm and stuffed it into his bag. "The Baron said this box belongs to his sister Kore, whose temple stands at the end of this trail. He said we must put it into her hands and that is what we will do."

The authority in his voice surprised me.

"Let us pass," Sam demanded. "Let us continue on our journey."

I waited for the wrath of this dark guardian glowering at us. He slapped his ankh against his thigh. Then he turned and disappeared into the fog, following Wolf and his pack, leaving us alone to face whatever was to come.

PART III KORE’S TEMPLE

CHAPTER 28

Sam and I gazed into the mist. We were alone. In unison, we took a step forward. Then another. I expected a response from the silent forest beyond the haze that surrounded us, but none came. As we walked, the fog pulled itself away and back into the woods until it was again flimsy ghosts.

After some time, we went around a bend and saw Kore's Temple at the top of the last climb. Sam and I stopped and sucked in our breath. We were almost there — after the challenges of the forest. He squeezed my hand.

Between where we stood and the entrance, a steep trail zigzagged up the mountain. The soft greens of living trees surrounded it. What an exquisite contrast to the grays of the Nether Realm behind us.

We hadn't been climbing long before the path narrowed, and Sam dropped my hand and pushed me ahead. The path widened again when we arrived at the level ground that was the summit of the mountain and the home of Kore's Temple. I grabbed Sam's hand and we walked together. Ahead, a stone bridge crossed a moat. On the other side was another impenetrable barrier with no doorway. Did this wall, like the one in The Baron's palace, have a hidden entrance?

Sam squeezed my hand and we walked forward. As we crossed the midpoint of the bridge, a door swung open. A small, elfish-looking man stepped out.

"Welcome, welcome," he squeaked, his voice a high falsetto. "To what do we owe the pleasure of your company?"

He wore a simple tunic and trousers but instead of white, his were a garish combination of pinks and purples. Where my tunic had a short V-neck exposing the top of my chest, his was deeply cut. It was similar to The Baron's shirt. He had a softer, almost childlike body.

His greeting surprised me. Everybody we had met on our journey knew who we were and why we were on our way to this temple.

Sam recovered faster than I did. "My name is Sam," he bowed, "and this is Sara."

"Yes, yes," the little man said. "Everyone is a Sam or a Sara. Why are you here?"

Sam tried again. "We have come from Empyrean, from the palace of The Baron."

"Of course, of course." The gatekeeper bounced on his toes. He wore elfish slippers — also pink and purple — with long pointed tips and small bells that tinkled when he moved. "There isn't anywhere else to be from. Now, tell me why are you here, Sam and Sara?"

In his slow, deliberate manner Sam continued. "The Baron has entrusted us with a gift, a gift for Kore, the Queen of the Dead."

"Oh." The man jumped behind the door. "Wait here." He disappeared. The opening slammed shut and again the wall was impenetrable.

Sam looked at me and shrugged. Was this our last challenge before we met the queen?

We waited for the gatekeeper to reappear. After a while, we turned and sat on the bridge. There was nowhere else to go and nothing else to do.

Finally, the door swung open and the little man peeked out. We jumped up and walked the few steps toward him.

"Stand back, stand back," he said. "Don't get too close."

We stopped an arm's distance away.

"Her high holiness, the Blessed, the great and glorious Queen of the Dead…" he paused, bowed his head, then clapped three times, "can't talk to you. Come back later."

He moved behind the door but before he could close it, Sam stepped forward and grabbed his arm. "Stop!" He pulled the little man out. "We've come a long way and have faced much to bring The Baron's gift to Kore, the Queen of the Dead. We have to meet with her."

"Yes, yes," the gatekeeper freed himself. "Wait here." He slammed the door shut again.

This time we didn't stand there looking at the blank wall but moved back to the bridge. The river below our feet was deep and clear.

As I watched the water, I noticed what looked like tiny baby dolls carried downstream by the rushing cascade. I wondered if this stream flowed through the canyon that had blocked us earlier. Would we have found piles of toys at the bottom of that ravine?

After another long wait, the door opened a third time.

"Her high holiness, the Blessed One, the great and glorious Mistress…" he paused, bowed his head, then clapped three times, "has agreed to see you."

He swung the portal open. We stepped into a shadowy passageway. I expected flickering torches hanging on the walls but there was no obvious light source. As soon as the door closed, the little man turned and pushed us into a side alcove.

"You look so dangerous." His high voice broke on the last syllable. "You must leave your weapons here."

I looked at Sam. He shrugged, removed the belt holding his dagger and its sheath, and set them on the rough wooden bench. I wanted to protest, remembering the times I pulled my weapon during our journey through the Nether Realm. But we had reached our goal. Surely, nothing would attack us here, so I followed his lead. We stood side-by-side in our tunics and trousers. I felt exposed, almost naked.

The little man smiled and clapped his hands as though we had completed a great performance.

"Follow me." He led us back into the dingy passageway, the tiny bells on his slippers adding an incongruous merry tone.

At the far end, he pushed against the wall and another door opened.

For a moment bright yellow sunlight bouncing off the columns blinded me. After our time in the dark, gray forest I had almost forgotten what sunshine looked like.

I turned to Sam. He was grinning. The pleasure of being away from the Nether Realm glowed through him.

The gatekeeper danced around on the balls of his feet, his bells tinkling.

"Yes, yes." He chuckled. "Isn't our temple gorgeous?"

It was stunning. A series of steps led up to the building. It reminded me of photos I had seen of the Parthenon. Everything was made of gleaming white marble with tiny flecks of mica that twinkled in the sunlight.

I stepped toward the stairs.

"No, no." The gatekeeper touched my arm. "You said you had a gift for the Great Queen." He bowed his head, then clapped three times. "Where is it?"

"We must deliver it to Kore herself." Sam's wariness was plain.

"Oh, of course, of course," the little man agreed, "but I need to see it."

Sam looked at me. I nodded. We were so close. We could not let this strange little man turn us away now. Besides, we knew no one could take the box. We had to give it to them.

Sam pulled The Baron's box out of his bag. It wiggled in his hand, pointing this way and that like an excited child.

The gatekeeper reached out as if to touch it, but Sam yanked it back. "Please, lead us to the Queen of the Dead."

"Yes, yes." The gatekeeper nodded. He pointed to another wooden bench along the barrier behind us. "You can leave the rest of your things there."

When we hesitated, he said, "You won't need those."

He was right. We left our bags on the bench.

The little man led us, skipping across the plaza that separated the temple from the wall that surrounded it. He bounded up the stairs, taking some of them two at a time.

The gatekeeper waited within the line of columns. "Her high holiness, the Blessed One, the great and glorious Mistress…" again he bowed his head, then clapped three times, "has agreed to meet with you. Please maintain a respectful attitude." He gestured. "Come, come."

Sam and I grabbed each other's hands. This was it, the moment we'd been working so hard to get to, our audience with Kore, the Queen of the Dead.

The little man, dancing to the tune of his own bells, led us to a hallway and into a small alcove. Tunics and trousers hung on pegs on either side of the room. Most were in bad condition, stained and torn.

"You can't meet the great and glorious Mistress…" he bowed his head, then clapped three times, "like that." He wrinkled his nose. "Take off those nasty things."

I looked down at myself, then at Sam. Our tunics weren't in much better shape than those around us. The gatekeeper's bells jangled as he tapped his toes.

"Hurry, hurry," he said. "The great and glorious Mistress…" again he bowed his head, then clapped three times, "is waiting."

I turned my back to the two men, and slipped out of my tunic and trousers, and hung them on an open peg. Looking at myself, I noticed that the small breasts and hips I had when I first arrived at Empyrean had vanished. I was now as flat and hairless as a child. I looked around for clean clothes but there were none.

"Come, come," the gatekeeper said. "Don't be shy, we've seen it all before."

I turned to look at Sam, standing naked beside me. He had also reverted to a child's androgynous body.

He picked up The Baron's box and reached out to me. I took a deep breath, slipping my hand into his.

The gatekeeper touched the far wall, and it swung open. I had expected the great queen's audience chamber to be at least as opulent as that of The Baron. But it was another dark hallway. Perhaps our escort was taking us to a dressing room where we could get more appropriate clothing.

As soon as we stepped through the opening, the door swung shut. I jumped when it latched with a ponderous finality. We followed the little man through the dim corridor. It was cold and musty. For the first time since leaving The Baron's palace I noticed the loose dirt beneath my bare feet. It had a spongy texture, damp but not muddy. The air smelled old, moldy with an under-scent like something dead was rotting in the walls.

The downward slope of the corridor became more pronounced the farther we went. Although I could not see more than a foot in any direction, I felt the weight of the earth above us. The passageway twisted and turned. There were many junctions with subsidiary hallways. At first I tried to remember our route, right, left, two rights, and so on, but soon gave up the effort.

I knew wherever we were going, we would not return this way. As we walked, I noticed the ceiling was sloping at a steeper angle than the floor. As the tallest person in the group I could sense the top of the passage brushing the top of my head. I felt like I needed to slouch.

We came to another dead end. A simple wooden door opened into a small alcove with benches on two sides. "Sit, sit," the gatekeeper said. "Her high holiness, the Blessed One, the great and glorious Mistress..." once more he bowed his head, then clapped three times, "will see you soon."

Sam and I sat down. The bench was cold on my bare skin and slick as though it had a thin coating of mildew.

"Ew." I recoiled.

"Sit. Down." Suddenly the gatekeeper's voice was deeper, more commanding. "When she's ready the great and glorious Mistress..." he bowed his head, and clapped three times, "will see you."

I looked at Sam, who shrugged. We had no choice. We were just two naked people at the mercy of this buffoon. I gritted my teeth and sat next to my compeer so that our hips, thighs, and knees touched.

The gatekeeper slammed the wooden door shut behind him.

Was this the end of our journey? Naked and alone, locked in this tiny room together? Would this be where we spent eternity?

CHAPTER 29

"It's been a long strange journey, hasn't it?" I took Sam's hand.

He nodded. It felt like an ending, arriving here, waiting to give The Baron's present to the great queen. What would we do afterward? Where could we go? What would become of us? What had Aurora told me? She'd said Empyrean was a way station, a place to help me remember before moving on. Had she meant our journey through the Nether Realm? Was there more, now that we had made it to Kore's Temple and would soon meet its queen? Would she send us back to the Nether Realm or even back to Empyrean? Perhaps we could stay here, in the bright, airy temple above.

Before I had a chance to share my thoughts with Sam, a wooden door in the opposite wall swung open. A guard in full Valkyrie battle gear, winged helmet, silver breastplate, long sword on her hip and a spear in one hand, stepped into the room.

She handed each of us a white sheet. We helped each other wrap them around ourselves, sarong-style. When we finished, Sam, holding The Baron's box in one hand, took my hand with his other.

"Her high holiness, the Blessed One, the great and glorious Mistress…" like the gatekeeper, she paused and bowed her head, "vil see you now."

The Valkyrie turned toward the open door, led us through and then stepped aside.

"Ereshkigal, Great Lady of the Earth, First Minister, the great and glorious Mistress," she intoned as we entered a magnificent audience room.

Not Kore. Someone else was standing between us and the completion of our journey. My face flushed with anger and disappointment. We'd come all this way, made it to Kore's Temple but here we were presented to another guardian. What was happening?

I surveyed the space as the Valkyrie marched us, hands entwined, to the foot of the oversized throne and pushed us into a respectful kneeling position with our foreheads to the floor. There wasn't much to see. The walls and the floor were the same gray stone with a slick damp sheen. There were no fancy rugs or tapestries here. It was hard surfaces except for the throne in front of us.

The chair was oversized and expansive, covered with layers of fabrics in rich dark colors. Its back rose high above the woman's head and ended in a sculpture of a cobra, hood flared, fangs extended. Wide-eyed owls formed the legs, while a pair of stuffed panthers stood as footstools in front.

Ereshkigal also appeared larger-than-life, wearing an elaborately embroidered cloak over an equally elaborately embroidered gown. The blood red hues of her clothing stood in stark contrast to the fabric of the throne and emphasized her deathly pale complexion. Her raven-black hair was pulled into braids and curls that had been shaped into an intricate pyramidal form on the top of her head.

She looked angry.

I heard the tinkle of tiny bells. It sounded like the gatekeeper had returned.

"Neti." The woman's frigid, bloodless voice filled the room, echoing off the stone walls, "Why have you disturbed us during our time of mourning?"

"Your high holiness, Blessed One, oh great and glorious Mistress…" he paused and then clapped three times, "they come from the forest of the Nether Realm. They come bearing a gift from your brother, The Baron, ruler of Empyrean. They insisted that they must see you, oh Great One. They would not be deterred."

"A gift, a gift from my brother. My brother who styles himself The Baron, ruler of the great fields of Empyrean? Where is this great gift from the land of sun and shade?"

The Valkyrie touched the tip of her spear against my buttocks. I wanted to protest. I wanted to protest everything that had happened to us since coming to this place, but I didn't. Perhaps if we satisfied this tyrant, we could speak to Kore, who the Baron said would guide us to the next phase of our journey in this dreadful afterlife.

I sat back on my heels. I noticed Sam did as well. He held The Baron's box on his lap.

The woman looked at us for a long moment. "They come from Empyrean?"

"So they say, Great One," Neti, the gatekeeper said. "So they say."

"And that small box is the gift from my great brother, the ruler of that place?"

"So they say, Great One," Neti said again, "so they say."

"Well, take it and send them on their way." Ereshkigal's irritation was obvious to everyone.

"As you well know, oh Blessed One, I cannot. They must give it to me." He paused and bowed his head. He turned toward us, smirking. Then he faced the woman again. "And they have refused to do so."

"Refused? Refused?" Ereshkigal stood. From where we sat she looked enormous. Her anger sat like a storm cloud on her bloodless face. "These simple souls, that you have stripped of what little my brother, The Great Baron, allowed them to bring into my realm." She came down the steps and stood looking at us. I felt like an insect about to be crushed. "These souls," she continued, "have refused to deliver his gift?"

The gatekeeper had moved aside. Now, he stepped farther away, as though wary of the anger of his mistress. "Yes, oh great and glorious One" He paused and clapped three times. "They have refused, they have refused to do so."

Ereshkigal looked at us. "Well, give it to me, then." She held out her hands to Sam.

After a moment's hesitation, he raised the box from his lap.

"No." I pushed my fear into the depths of my stomach. "The Baron said this box belonged to his sister, Kore. And you are not her." Out of the corner of my eye, I saw Sam settle the box back onto his lap, covering it with both hands. "We have come a long way and endured much to bring this box back to its rightful owner. If you will allow us to give it to Kore, who The Baron called the Queen of the Dead, you can to return to the mourning we have interrupted."

Sam turned to stare at me. I was as shocked as he was. How could I be so audacious?

"I am the Ereshkigal, first Minister to Kore, the Queen of the Dead"

"Your high holiness, you are the Blessed One. You are the great and wondrous Ereshkigal. "The gatekeeper took a breath and then clapped his hand three times. "You," he continued, "are the glorious First Minister."

"Give The Baron's box to me." Ereshkigal held out both hands to Sam, ignoring me.

This was not her box, I thought. Why did she think he would give it to her? I laid my hand on Sam's arm, reminding him of our agreement as compeers.

"No, your highness," he moaned. "The Baron commanded us to deliver this to Kore." I heard him swallow. "We cannot give it to you." He looked down, no longer caught in the power of her glance.

There was a long silence.

"Remove them." Ereshkigal waved her arm to dismiss us and then turned away. Before any one moved, she turned back and smiled — a diabolical and malicious smile. "No." She looked behind us at her gatekeeper. "If he won't cooperate, let him hang on the wall until, until…" We waited while she considered. "Let him hang forever, Neti. Let my brother come looking for him if he dares."

She turned and disappeared behind the throne.

At first nothing happened and then I felt the Valkyrie's spear point against my back.

"Stand up, up" the gatekeeper said, his voice no longer so high pitched but low, commanding. He stood in front of Sam.

"Hold out your hands," he ordered. "Hold them out."

Sam obeyed, still clutching The Baron's box. The Valkyrie wrapped a leather thong around and around his hands, cocooning them around The Baron's box. When the Valkyrie stepped away, Sam collapsed into a heap on the floor. Had he fainted? I turned toward him. Before I could move, a muscular man in warrior's garb like that of the Valkyrie's picked up Sam's body. He carried it to the wall opposite the Ereshkigal's throne. There he draped the leather thong over a meat hook. Sam's arms were stretched over his head and his toes almost touched the floor.

"No!" I ran to where Sam's inert body hung on the wall. "You can't do this."

"Silence," the gatekeeper commanded. "If you know what's good for you, you will not disturb her high holiness, the Blessed One, the great and glorious Mistress." He paused, bowed his head and clapped three times. "You don't want her coming back here."

"Keep them quiet," he told the Valkyrie. Then he touched a secret spot on the wall and walked through the door that swung open, leaving me alone with Sam's body.

After a moment, the throne and the steps leading up to it rose. When the whole thing stood a foot above the surrounding floor, it rotated. I watched fascinated as Ereshkigal's throne disappeared and a faceless stone wall came into view. When everything settled back, it left us in a featureless room with no visible means of escape.

CHAPTER 30

There was no time in this afterlife. No days or weeks or months, no hours, or minutes, or seconds. Sam hung from the slimy wall of Ereshkigal's audience room like a slab of meat in a third-world market. I sat at his feet in the posture of abject mourning. We had come so far together and now he was truly dead and I was too distraught to consider whether there was a way to escape this latest challenge.

The Baron had said when we gave the box to Kore she would guide us along to the next phase of our journey. But it was obvious we had made a wrong turn and fallen into the clutches of Ereshkigal and her gatekeeper. There was no help for us. What would have happened if we had given her the box? It would not have been good. She could have taken The Baron's casket and still put us in this same situation.

Our Valkyrie guard stood as still as a marble statue. Was she guarding us from the rescuers who would not come or was she there to assure that we didn't formulate an escape plan?

Had we walked into a trap that left us captured and Sam trussed up and hung on this wall? No one except the great and glorious minister and her miniature gatekeeper knew where we were. And she was willing to leave us hanging here, for… for… I screamed into the emptiness, "How long is forever in this wretched place?"

As if on cue, a door opened and in skipped Neti, the bells on his slippers tinkling. What looked like the cleaning crew, three people with buckets, mops, and rags, followed him. Ignoring us, they swabbed the floor and walls. They were naked and sexless as children although they were the size of adults. They carried out their duties with the diligence of good servants with Neti following behind first one and then another, pointing out spots they missed. However, the buckets were filled with filthy water and their rags added instead of removed dirt. I watched speechless as they left every part of the room with a thin sheen of mildew and mud.

As they were leaving, the gatekeeper turned to glare at us. "Them, too."

Without a flicker of recognition of our status as people like themselves, the cleaning crew — or perhaps I should call them the griming crew — brought their buckets over to Sam and me. They pulled off his sheet. Starting with his feet, they slathered muck up his legs, over his bare torso, and up his arms. One stood me up and released my sarong. While two held me tight, another used a filthy rag to cover me head to toe with the dirty water. The Neti watched, smirking as I twisted and turned, trying to avoid their touch.

When at last Sam and I were both covered with sludge, the gatekeeper clapped as though the workers had provided an award-winning performance.

One worker picked up the sheet that had fallen to the floor and wrapped it around me. It was as disgusting as I was, cold and wet, soaked with the foul water.

"Wait," I said as Neti and his crew turned toward the door. "You can't leave us like this."

The gatekeeper looked back. "Will you give me the box entrusted to you by The Baron, the self-styled ruler of Empyrean?"

"I-I can't," I whispered.

"Then, I do as her high holiness, the Blessed One, the great and glorious minister," he paused, bowed his head, and clapped three times, "says." He followed his crew through the door.

I shivered as though my body had been dipped into an icy stream. I wept, my cries echoing off the stone walls surrounding us.

When I had no more tears, I realized something had changed.

The Valkyrie was gone, and she had left the door ajar. I stood and crept across the room. I needed to let Kore know we were here. This was her temple. At least, I thought it was. Someone had to know how to contact her.

I peeked through the doorway. Beyond was a long corridor not too different from the one that led us here. Light from the room behind me illuminated it for a short way but the walls beyond glowed.

I turned back to look at Sam's body hanging on the wall. I could see the bulge between his hands where he held The Baron's box. The only other thing left from our journey was the leather thong I tied around his wrist. I twisted the matching strip tied on my wrist and I remembered what we had told each other, "We are more than companions, more than friends, more than family. We are compeers… forever."

I looked at the corridor beckoning me and then back at Sam hanging on the far wall. We had been together since The Baron placed his box in our hands.

I stared down the passageway, twisting the leather strap around my wrist. Perhaps I could escape, although I did not know where I could go. Not to the Nether Realm or to Empyrean. Maybe I could find Kore. Wasn't this her temple? I wasn't abandoning Sam. Was I? I could come back for him. Couldn't I?

After a long time, I returned to my place below Sam's body. I couldn't release him and I wouldn't leave him. It looked like a bleak eternity but we were compeers. We'd spend it here together.

CHAPTER 31

I don't know how long I continued to sit against the wall. It may have been an hour or an eternity. The room was dirty, cold and smelled of mold and slime. I was dirty and cold. I smelled awful, too.

Then our Valkyrie pushed a door open. Another group of workers followed her. They wore tunics and trousers like those we had on when we first approached this vile place. Theirs were the pastel colors of spring flowers, yellow and pink and baby blue. They carried buckets and mops and rags.

I groaned, still miserable from the ministrations of the earlier crew. It was such a small thing, but I was not ready to face the gatekeeper and his petty tortures. Like a child, I closed my eyes, hoping to make myself invisible, listening to the workers as they moved around the room.

When my curiosity overcame my fear, I slit my eyes open. This group ignored Sam and me and the Valkyrie who stood nearby. Instead, they swabbed the floors and walls. They appeared cheerful, whispering and talking together. After a moment, I realized that they were cleaning everything rather than making it dirtier. They kept switching out buckets of dirty water for fresh clean ones. They washed away the grime and dirt left by the other crew. We were still underground, but it felt as if sunlight had penetrated into this room. It brightened and become warmer.

Two of them pressed a secret lever. A part of the floor rose, then rotated. The wall disappeared and a new throne came into view. The same size as Ereshkigal's throne, it was made from a light, gleaming wood. Blooming trees, flowers, and even tiny birds covered it. Although the birds were carved into the arms and legs of the chair, they seemed to move and sing, like the decorations stores put up during the winter holidays.

At last the leader of the cleaning crew appeared to notice us. "What's this?" She walked over to the Valkyrie. "Did the Blessed One Ereshkigal leave these?"

The guard nodded. "They have been awaiting your arrival."

The woman clapped like a small child on Christmas morning. "Wonderful. These must be the latest from Queen's brother, The Baron, ruler of Empyrean. The great and glorious Kore so loves when these arrive."

Then she came to Sam. Her white tunic was pristine. Although she'd been working along with the others, hers appeared freshly laundered. I thought she must find us disgusting. We were both filthy. We looked and smelled like we had been playing in a sewer. I wanted to greet her, complain about our treatment, but I was too dispirited to speak.

The woman did not seem surprised at our condition. She didn't wrinkle her nose in disgust or say anything to us. Instead she called to two of the workers, "Clean up these babies. They're filthy. But be careful of the thong tying his hands together. Don't let it break or unwind."

With that, one worker grabbed Sam around his waist and lifted him until they could slip his wrists off the meat hook. They laid him on the floor. Then they moved his arms from over his head and rubbed them. Their touch was gentle, warm, the opposite of how we had been treated by Ereshkigal and her minions. Sam's eyes fluttered open.

"*Querida.*" He smiled at me. "Are you all right?"

I nodded, then pulled him to me, wrapping my arms around him. My Sam had returned.

Other workers brought buckets of water and clean rags and washed us. It felt heavenly. Was our luck changing? The Valkyrie observed the whole process. I expected her to protest or notify Ereshkigal's gatekeeper, but she didn't move or show any expression.

When we were clean, they dried us. The woman who appeared in charge watched them wrap us in matching clean, white sheets. Sam cleared his throat. "The Baron gave us a box. He said belonged to Kore, the Queen of the Dead. He sent us here to give it to her."

"But —" I wanted to tell this woman the whole story. To tell her what we had endured in the forest of the Nether Realm, how we had been treated since arriving here at Kore's Temple.

"Yes, yes," she interrupted me. "The Blessed Kore has been away, and so you were brought to her sister Ereshkigal instead. That often happens. The Blessed Kore will know what to do with you and with your gift." Her smile brightened the room, and I swallowed my complaints. It didn't matter anymore.

She led us to a rug placed at the foot of the new throne. It reminded me of a living forest on either side of a great river. We knelt in the center with its shades of blue. The outer borders were abstract greens and browns with splashes of reds and yellows. As we had done so many times before, we bowed, placing our heads to the floor. I was surprised Sam didn't appear stiff or sore from his time hanging on the wall. The woman wrapped another sheet around the two of us, bundling us together into a single package. I felt the warmth of Sam's hips and thighs touching mine.

The rug was soft and clean. I'm sure our pose was meant to be servile, as it had when we were forced into a similar state at the foot of both The Baron's and Ereshkigal's throne. Now it felt comfortable. Our posture reminded me of the child's pose in Yoga because of its similarity to a fetal position. I was warm and snug.

The workers gathered up their things, and then it was silent. Perhaps the Valkyrie was still there guarding us, but I didn't care. Warm and dry and comfortable, I could spend my afterlife beneath this sheet, nestled up to Sam. I closed my eyes and drifted toward sleep.

"What now?" Sam whispered.

I was startled out of my drowsy state. "I don't know. It looks like we will finally meet Kore, The Baron's other sister, the Queen of the Dead. We'll give her The Baron's grisly box and then, and then… who knows?"

I pushed my hand toward my compeer and his hands, still wrapped in the leather thong. What would happen now? Would we be sent into the forest of the Nether Realm or even to Empyrean? Neither returning to the world of Anubis or back to Volos and his workroom was appealing. I had discovered as much as I wanted to know about my previous life. I hadn't been a nice person but there was nothing I could do to change that or the death that brought me here. Had this been a test? A kind of Purgatory? We both knew what we had done and had at least tried to make amends to each other. I thought of everything we had endured in the forests of the Nether Realm and here at Kore's Temple. Had we suffered enough? Was this temple the entrance to heaven, the afterlife I'd heard about all my life? Or would Kore be our final judge? Sam had been a good man. His destination shouldn't be in doubt, but I was unsure about myself. I didn't deserve eternal damnation, but I did not deserve celestial bliss either.

"As long as we're together, *querida*." Sam's voice cut through my whirling thoughts. "I can do anything, go anywhere, endure anything as long as you are with me."

I smiled into the floor, my heart swollen with the feelings pent up there. No matter what, we would not allow them to separate us. Again, I realized I had made the right decision to stay here with Sam.

"Have I told you I love you, my beloved?" I asked. "I could never have made this journey without you."

"We could never have completed this journey without each other," he said. "I love you, too, *querida*."

Without even thinking, we scooted closer together, tightening the sheet around ourselves. We pressed into each other so that not only did our hands touch, but also our shoulders, hips and legs.

At that moment I would have been content to spend my eternity kneeling on this floor with Sam. But that was too much to ask. I heard the tinkling of the gatekeeper's bells. Was our time of peace and comfort coming to an end?

CHAPTER 32

By the sound of his bells, I followed the gatekeeper's path from somewhere behind the throne and down the steps until he stood to our left.

"Kore, Great Mistress of the Temple," he intoned in a rich, full voice that seemed at odds with his persona. "Seed of the Fruit of the Fields, Queen of the Dead," he clapped three times. Behind us a chorus of voices echoed him. "Kore, Great Mistress of the Temple, Seed of the Fruit of the Fields, Queen of the Dead." The tinkling of many tambourines surrounded us. I wanted to sit up and look around but dared not. Instead, I pushed closer to Sam.

"Shh, *querida*," he whispered.

The music stilled, but the room was not quiet. I heard rustling above and in front of us as well as behind us where the tambourine player stood.

"What is this?" The voice from the throne sounded warm. It flowed like honey that held all the beauty of summer.

"Your brother, The Baron, ruler of Empyrean has sent these two souls to you, Great Queen." The gatekeeper's obeisant tone shouldn't have surprised me but it did.

"New souls." I heard the pleasure in the Great Queen's voice as she clapped like a small child. "Please unwrap them for me, Daena."

As the sheet was pulled away from our heads, the woman who had cleaned and wrapped us whispered, "Sit up, darlings."

When we raised our heads, the woman removed the sheet and rearranged our sarongs. We sat, thighs touching, my hand resting on Sam's bound hands.

Like her sister Ereshkigal, Kore appeared larger-than-life. She wore an elaborately embroidered cloak over an equally elaborately embroidered gown. Images of fruit and flowers, birds and the many small creatures of the forest covered her gown and her cloak. Both garments were made from a shimmering pale yellow silk that accented her fair hair and creamy complexion.

Her smile warmed and comforted me.

"Neti." The queen's soft voice filled the room. "Unbind his hands. Let's see what my brother, The Baron, has sent."

A man I didn't recognize stepped in front of us and unwound the thongs from Sam's hand. The Neti we had met earlier had been a small, elfish man, but this one was tall and muscular. He appeared to be hairless. His head, eyebrows, and even his arms and his chest were smooth as though freshly shaven. His trousers and tunic were a swirl of yellows and oranges with a hint of a rosy pink. The only resemblance he had with the Neti we knew were the elfish slippers with the long pointed toes and tiny bells.

I rested my hand on Sam's thigh as this new Neti released his hands. When he finished, Sam held The Baron's box on his lap. I considered putting my own hands in my lap but left the one on Sam's thigh.

"My box," the great queen cried. "He sent it back." She clapped her hands again like a small child being offered a special toy.

Sam held the box out toward her but she did not seem eager to take it.

"First, tell me what my brother, the ruler of Empyrean, told you about this wondrous thing."

"He said it was yours and he was using us to return it." Sam looked straight at the great queen without a hint of deference. "He said when we returned it, you would guide us along to the next phase of our journey."

"Of course, of course I will, dear ones." Again her smile filled the room with sunshine and the smell of a spring garden.

"And you." She turned to me. "You seem to think your quest has been a kind of punishment."

How did she know my most secret thoughts? "Yes, my queen," I tried to keep the anger I felt out of my voice. Nothing would be served by antagonizing this guardian who had already been so kind to us.

She smiled and nodded as if encouraging me to continue.

"When I first realized I was dead, I thought I was in heaven or maybe the anteroom of heaven."

"But then you discovered otherwise, didn't you, dear one?"

"Empyrean was no heaven," I said, perhaps too strongly, "and neither was the Nether Realm."

"But neither were they hell, as we understand it, great one." Sam interrupted my story.

The great queen smiled. "It has been difficult, hasn't it, dear ones?"

Sam and I nodded. "Yes, ma'am." He spoke for the two of us. I bit back the angry words that threatened this pleasant conversation.

"And what have you learned?" the Kore asked.

Without turning my head, I looked toward the new gatekeeper next to me.

"You may speak freely," he said. How did these people know what I was thinking? "No one will hurt you here."

I did not trust that our torment had ended, but what else could they do now? I decided to tell the truth as I had discovered it.

"I wasn't a nice person when I was alive." Shame heated my cheeks. "I was arrogant and cruel to the people under me, focused on myself and my career. I used my friends, lovers, and employees. Then, when they were no longer useful, I discarded them."

The queen nodded. "Not unlike my sister, Ereshkigal" she murmured.

Looking at the floor, I realized I had been much like Ereshkigal. "I created great suffering among those like my beloved, who you people call Sam." I turned and smiled at him. He had forgiven me for the anguish I had caused him, including both of our deaths, but I had not expunged my guilt.

"And you?" The queen's attention returned to Sam.

"If the one-you-call-Sara," he smiled at me, "was unkind when she was alive, I was too compliant. I let other people — my wife, my family and friends, and, of course, my bosses — use and abuse me. If I'd had more backbone, I might never have been standing on my former boss's porch the night we both died."

"Are you different now?" she asked us.

I nodded. "The-one-you-call-Sam has taught me how to love and care. I've learned that not every story is about me. Yes, I think I am a different person now."

"And I've learned how to stand up for myself and my beloved," Sam said, his voice strong. "We made it here to your temple, great queen, because we worked together, calling on both our strengths." He turned to smile at me. "She didn't even abandon me as I hung on that wall. She could have but waited with me instead. We've become a superb team."

"That you have," said Kore, the Mistress of the Temple and Queen of the Dead. Her smile disappeared. Her stern expression reminded me of her sister Ereshkigal. "Now it is time for you to continue your journey."

Here it comes, I thought, the end of the niceties and back to the torment of this place they called the Bardo.

CHAPTER 33

The voice of the woman who cleaned and wrapped us earlier, the one the great queen called Daena, pushed us. "Stand up, children," she whispered. As we rose, the sheet fell away. There was a soft murmur behind us when Sam's hand found mine as we waited for this queen to declare our next torture.

"Yes, yes," the queen said as though responding not to us but to the murmurs of those we could not see. "You are right, we must keep them together." She stared for a moment and nodded as if making a decision. Then she turned away.

"Wait," Sam cried out, stopping her before she disappeared behind the throne. He had developed courage. "Don't you want your box?" He dropped my hand and held The Baron's gift out to her with two hands, as though it was an offering.

The great queen turned back toward us. "Oh, yes. My box. Of course." She smiled. "There is a great treasure for you in that box but you need to keep it for a while longer. Please be careful with it. I will claim it soon."

I stared as she disappeared behind the throne. There was a great treasure for us in the box? We had met Kore, the Queen of the Dead to whom The Baron said we must deliver the box. But after everything we had been through, now when we could give it to its rightful owner, the great queen was refusing it. Now she was saying she didn't want the thing, that we should keep it and guard it while we endured whatever new torture she was planning. For a short while, I had thought Kore, this Queen of the Dead was different from the other guardians. Different from The Baron and his minions, Volos, and Aurora, and Sigrún. Different from Anubis, the deer-men, and the cat-men who tried to deflect us from our mission. Different from Ereshkigal, and her sadistic gatekeeper. Now I knew I was wrong.

Red-hot anger flooded me. I wanted to protest, to wail and stamp my feet. I wanted to grab the thing out of Sam's hands and throw it at the queen's retreating form or smash it against the floor.

Before I could act, Sam palmed the box and grabbed my hand. I'm sure he felt the heat of my frustration flowing up his arm and into his torso.

"Hush, *querida*," he said, his voice quiet, soothing. He was trying to tame me as he had tamed the wolf.

As fast as it came, my anger flowed away, replaced by tears seeping out of my eyes and down my cheeks. I thought we had reached the end of our journey. I never considered that this queen who appeared so gentle and kind would refuse to accept The Baron's gift.

There was no sign that the other people in this audience room noticed my anger. Instead, the new Neti turned to the woman standing behind us. "Bring them." He opened a new doorway.

Leaving the sheet that covered us at our feet, Daene grabbed my free hand and pulled me after her. "Come along, dear ones."

There was nothing for us to do but to follow. As we approached the doorway, I noticed the words "Remember, Release, Return" engraved above it. It reminded me of the door leading from The Baron's palace to the Nether Realm. Neti and Daena led us into another passage. The walls glowed the color of a fairy woodland at dawn. We could barely see where we were going. I heard the steady drip of water from somewhere in front of us. The passageway was wide enough for Sam and me to walk shoulder-to-shoulder, hand-in-hand. While the floor sloped upward, taking us ever higher, the ceiling faded away. The passage felt light and airy.

After we walked for some time, this new Neti stepped aside. "You can find your way from here." He nodded down the passageway. Since I had not seen a single intersection, his statement was unnecessary. Even though there was nowhere to go but forward, I tried to pull back. I wanted to refuse to continue, but Daena again grabbed my free hand to pull us forward. I felt like a small child being towed along by a heedless parent.

The passageway made a sharp ninety-degree turn, and we were standing behind a curtain of water. Although I could not see beyond the waterfall, I sensed a large open area filled with soft yellow light.

"Don't be afraid," Deana said. "You both have been brave and devoted to each other. Your new life is through there."

"Hold out your hands. Ah, good, good." She fiddled with the leather thongs we had wrapped around our wrists. When she stepped back, she had tied the two straps into a single band. "This will help keep you together." She smiled when she noticed we had not loosened our grip on each other's hands. Then she pushed us through the waterfall.

CHAPTER 34

Beyond the waterfall was an oasis. We stood on a granite ledge mere feet above a clear, turquoise-blue pool surrounded by a sandy beach complete with palm trees and colored birds. Above and behind us, Kore's temple rose, a gleaming white structure of pillars and shadows. Below stood people in tunics and trousers in all the colors of the rainbow. I could see the guardians we had met along our journey, including Aurora and Sigrún, Ankou and Volos, The Baron, Anubis and Wolf, and even Ereshkigal with her gatekeeper Neti. They were singing and dancing when we passed through the water. Then they became quiet with the shimmer of tambourines and the echo of drums floating over the water. They smiled at us. Volos had that look fathers get when their children have won an important prize. Ereshkigal still looked stern but no longer terrifying. Her Neti bounced as though he could not control his excitement. All the people's happy faces suggested a wonderful event was about to take place.

The water fell behind us, ran across the ledge, and into the pool. It tickled the bottom of my feet. And there she was, Kore, Great Mistress of the Temple, Seed of the Fruit of the Fields, Queen of the Dead. She had sloughed off most of her royal regalia and was wearing a simple pale yellow gown. Like us, she was barefoot, the hem of her dress skimming the top of the water as it flowed along. Her Neti stood on a dry portion behind and above her. When I looked at him, he smiled, not the sinister smirk I expected but a warm and welcoming smile that rose from his lips to his eyes. It made him appear more like a grandfather than the frightening gatekeeper we met earlier.

Without a word Kore embraced the two of us. She seemed unconcerned that we were soaking wet from our step through the waterfall. "Welcome at last," she said when she released her hold and held us at arm's length. Her look was appraising as though she had not seen enough in the audience room.

"Now you may give me the gift from my brother The Baron, the ruler of Empyrean." She smiled and then pressed our hands together. "You have done well to guard this so we might have it as you two begin your final quest."

Sam and I brought our free hands up and held the box as we had received it from The Baron. When we presented it to the great queen, she clapped, bouncing like a small child receiving a much-anticipated present. Even the box wiggled in expectation of the exchange. She took it and lifted it over her head for those on the beach below us to see. They erupted in wild applause and cheering, along with the sounds of tambourines and drums pounding.

I wondered what she meant by our great quest. We had been on a journey at least since we left The Baron's palace and perhaps since the moment we each arrived in the Bardo. Where were we to go now? Did this queen have another assignment, a new quest to challenge us? I sighed, exhausted and not ready for another ordeal. Sam squeezed my hand. I squeezed back. As long as we could stay together all would be well.

The gatekeeper made a sign and the cheering and applause stilled.

"Your time with us is coming to a close." Kore turned toward Daena who had come through the waterfall and stood behind us. "I see you have tied these two together."

"Their journey began together," Daena said, "even though they were separated by the times of their deaths. Your brother, The Baron, ruler of Empyrean, brought them back together for their passage through the Nether Realm. We've watched them grow on their way here to your Temple. As the Sam said in your audience room, they have become a team, and they wish to stay together."

The queen turned to us. "Is that true? You were brought together first by the circumstances of your deaths and then by The Baron's quest. Do you want to remain together, your spirits entwined for the whole of what is to come?"

When she smiled, I felt my anger drain away. Our journey through the Nether Realm taught me love and devotion for my Sam. I would never have asked for such challenges, but at that moment I realized it was the trials we endured that had changed and softened me. Our journey that had enabled me to love and be loved. The strength of Sam's love for me and mine for him flowed like sunlight between us.

I looked at Sam. He smiled at me.

"Yes," I said, "even if you unbound our hands, we would continue to hold on to each other, whatever is to come."

The Kore looked at my compeer.

He nodded. "Our hearts are one. Bound or unbound we will continue to hold each other, whatever comes."

The great queen squeezed our hands as though that pressure would more firmly bind us. Again the crowd below erupted in applause and cheers.

Kore dropped our hands and turned to Daena, holding The Baron's box out to her. Its incessant movement stopped, and it glowed in the light of this place.

Daena unlatched the little clasp and raised the lid. I held my breath. What wonder was inside this box we had protected since leaving The Baron's Palace?

I expected a miniature skeleton or another macabre memento. Instead I saw a tiny ruby and a small vial resting on a burgundy cushion. My shoulders slumped. After everything we had been through, I had expected something more impressive.

Kore took the jewel and snapped it in two. She opened Sam's sarong and let it fall to his feet. Then she pressed one piece of the ruby into his chest above his heart. Turning to me she removed my cloth and then pressed the other piece into my chest. I felt a small flash of heat where the jewel touched me but no pain. I looked down. It had embedded itself into my skin.

Then she opened the vial and poured golden oil into her palm. She rubbed her hands together, then brought them first to my face and then to Sam's. With more oil, she massaged our necks, our arms, our torsos and backs, our legs and feet. Her touch soothed the pain of our journey through the Bardo, leaving a warm feeling of contentment and peace.

My memories of Empyrean, of Aurora and Sigrún, of my stint at the loom slipped away, becoming more and more unreal, as if they had been stories I had read somewhere. In the same way my memories of our adventures in the Nether Realm, of Wolf and his pack, of the deer-men and their cat-men followers, of Anubis and the time we spent trapped near the path became dim and ethereal. Even the horrors of Kore's temple, of Ereshkigal and her gatekeeper, of Sam hanging in the audience room faded into a distant memory. Our meeting with the great queen Kore, Daene and the second gatekeeper, our final journey to this pool, floated away on the subtle beat of the drums below us.

I squeezed Sam's hand. Kore's oil could make me forget, but I would not allow her to fail to remember my beloved. He returned my squeeze. Even if we forgot everything we had learned, everything we had become, we still had each other.

"Your time here is finished," the great queen said, interrupting my fall into oblivion. "Follow the light to your new life."

She stepped back. Strong hands pushed us forward and over the lip of the ledge. We tumbled into the pool.

Down, down we fell, deeper and deeper. I held my breath until my lungs burned, desperate for air. We had plunged far under the water. Was this our final death? Had everything we experienced been the hazy illusion of our dying brains? I opened my mouth, willing to endure my extinction. Water poured into my lungs. But I didn't die.

I felt a tugging on my wrist. Sam was pointing to a pure white light beckoning from below. Now freed from the desire to breathe, together we swam toward the future promised by the great queen Kore, Mother of all Life.

EPILOGUE

Arizona Republic
March 28, 2011
Rare twins born holding hands.
A set of rare twins were born holding hands at the University Medical Center yesterday. The boys, Daniel and David Conlan, born March 27, are rare monoamniotic or "mono mono" identical twins.
This means they shared an amniotic sac and were in constant contact during the pregnancy. Their condition meant that their mother Marilyn Conlan had to remain on bed rest for weeks at the University Medical Center. The twins had been monitored for months since mono mono twins can become entangled in each other's umbilical cords.
Thankfully for Conlan and her husband Ralph, their sons were born healthy at 33 weeks.
As the boys were born, doctors held them up over a sheet so that Conlan and her husband could see them. The newborns were holding hands. Each twin sported a tiny heart-shaped birthmark on his chest.
"I didn't think they would come out and instantly be holding hands. It was overwhelming. I can't even put it into words," Conlan said. "There wasn't a dry eye in the whole OR."

About the Author

Mary Ann Clark is both a published scholar and an explorer of speculative fiction.

Growing up on the high plains of Colorado, Mary Ann received her undergraduate degree from Creighton University, in Omaha, NE. She earned an MBA from the University of Houston, and started her own technical writing company. There she managed the writing of computer documentation and other types of procedure manuals.

After almost twenty years as a technical writer, Mary Ann went back to school to earn a Ph.D. in Religious Studies from Rice University, in Houston, Texas. Currently, she is a faculty member at Yavapai College in Prescott, Arizona where she teaches Comparative Religion.

As a recognized authority on the Afro-Caribbean religions, primarily Santería/Lukumi, she has published three academic books: *Then We Will Sing a New Song: African Influences on America's Religious Landscape* (Roman & Littlefield, 2012), *Santería: Correcting the Myths and Uncovering the Realities of a Growing Religion* (Praeger Publishers, 2007) and *Where Men are Wives and Mothers Rule: Santería Ritual Practices and Their Gender Implications* (University Press of Florida, 2005).

Her debut novella *The Baron's Box* is an account of one woman's journey through a surprising afterlife.

Connect with Mary Ann:

Blog: https://drmaryann.wordpress.com/musings/

Twitter: https://twitter.com/drmaryann

Facebook: https://www.facebook.com/mary.a.clark.395

Want to keep up with the latest Mary Ann Clark releases? Subscribe to her announcement list, http://eepurl.com/cVeMHf, to receive release-day alerts and news about special events and signings.

Made in the USA
San Bernardino, CA
31 January 2018